THE NIGHTMARE AWAKES

Dan carried his daughter down to the green-lit hell beneath his house. There he found his son, sealed within a box of glassy plastic.

Dan's hands removed the cords and tape from Millie, then his body was turned away and set to yet another task. His hands moved with easy familiarity to operate a latch that he had never seen before, and slid open a cabinet built in against the silo's curving walls. Inside the cabinet, motionless as a costume hanging in a closet, the crab-machine that had pursued him through three nights of dreaming horror stood upright on its hind pair of legs . . .

FRED SABERHAGEN
SPECIMENS

A TOM DOHERTY ASSOCIATES BOOK
NEW YORK

SPECIMENS

A Tor Book
Published by Tom Doherty Associates, Inc.
49 West 24th Street
New York, N.Y. 10010

Cover art by Wayne Barlowe

ISBN: 0-812-52579-5

First Tor edition: August 1990

Printed in the United States of America

0 9 8 7 6 5 4 3 2 1

▪ CHAPTER ▪

1

Looking from the high narrow windows in the southeastern bedroom, Dan Post could see a vague crescent of daytime moon. Far below it, on the horizon and some twenty-five miles from where he stood, the tallest building in the world was plainly visible along with two slightly lesser gods of Chicago's Loop. The eaves on the old suburban house were narrow, and even the high-latitude sun of summer could strike in under them to get at the glass in the old windows. The glass, mottled with wavy distortions, might be as old as the house itself. Dan thought he could see how the panes had begun to purple, like desert glass, from decade upon decade of the sun hurling its fire at them across ninety million miles of space.

He leaned back a little from the window and shifted his weight meditatively on the wide, solid planks of the old floor, which squeaked just very slightly as he did so. Dan was rather heavy but solid, a muscular man in his mid-thirties. A slightly concave nose gave him a somewhat boyish look. His hair was darkly unruly above a pale, tan-resistant face. Today he was dressed in double-knit slacks and sport shirt for looking at old houses in mid-June; he had to admit, though, that the upper floor of this vacant, air-conditionerless place wasn't as unmercifully hot as he had expected. There was an attic above, which helped, and the windows had been left slightly open. The place must catch every breeze: it was on the top of a fairly steep hill.

"So," he asked, "this house is supposed to be a hundred and forty years old?"

"That's right," Ventris, the real estate agent, was standing relaxed in the bedroom doorway. It was a big bedroom by modern standards, and the house had three more like it on its second floor, not one of them smaller than twelve feet by thirteen. A room or so away Nancy and the kids were discussing something in low voices.

"They say," Ventris continued, "that it used to be a way station on the Underground Railroad. You know, before the Civil War, when slaves were being smuggled north to Canada."

"Well, I suppose that's possible." Dan's interest was no more than polite. The house did not strike him as likely to be historically interesting, or even extremely old. The walls and woodwork in this bedroom had been painted light green not long ago, determinedly made new-looking by interior latex put on somewhat carelessly with a roller, leaving a few spatters on the worn but solid floor. Anyway, the railroad Dan was concerned about, the commuters' kind, ran through Wheatfield Park

2

about half a mile to the north of here, and according to Ventris the station was just over a mile away. Dan supposed that if he got up early every day and walked, it would help him keep in shape. Of course he could ride into the city with Nancy, who would be driving in anyway, as long as she kept her job . . . they would have to see how that worked out.

"Of course," Ventris added, "people tend to say that about any house this old, at least in this part of the country." While leading Dan and Nancy through two other houses earlier in the day, Ventris had shown himself to be very much the low-pressure type of salesman. Sandy-haired and paunchy, he seemed on the way to aging gracefully in the real estate business. He didn't look old enough to have got into it after retirement from something else.

"What was that about the Underground Railroad?" Nancy, wearing slacks and a summery blouse, now came with Dan's two children to join him in the southeast bedroom. The two kids were somewhat silent and thoughtful today, as if this business of looking at houses brought home to them forcefully the fact that their good pal Nancy was soon going to assume the office of motherhood over them. Millie was eleven and Sam was nine, and both of them had their father's sturdy frame and wild dark hair. But often, as now, when they were quiet and thoughtful, he could see their mother in their eyes. Cancer, a year and a half ago. The wounds of the survivor healed, the children changed and grew. Life went on, and the gonads like all the other organs kept working away, and now here he was, picking out another home in which to settle a new bride.

3

"My girl, the history nut." Dan put an arm around Nancy and squeezed her shoulders. "Mr. Ventris was just saying that this might have been a station, or whatever they called their stopping places. But never mind that; how would you like to live here?"

"There's certainly lots of room." Nancy brushed back her straight black hair. "But oh, it's such a hodgepodge." She was a rather tall girl, who towered over her little Japanese-born mother in Chicago, and was almost of a height with her American father and her husband-to-be. She was in her early twenties, years younger than Dan. "The downstairs looks like some decorator's sample case."

Today Nancy was evidently not going to be distracted by historical discoveries, but others might. Millie took her father's hand and looked around, and pondered aloud: "I wonder where they hid the slaves."

"Maybe the basement or the attic." This reminded Dan of another point he meant to check, and he walked out into the spacious upstairs hall and stood looking up at a closed trapdoor in the ceiling. "Is there a chair around somewhere?" he asked Ventris. "I'd like to take a look at the attic now if possible."

"I think there is. Let me check." Ventris moved away to rummage in a closet, and Dan rejoined Nancy and the kids in the southeast bedroom, where they were enjoying the view from the window.

"This is neat, being up on a hill," young Sammy commented.

"Not bad," Dan agreed. From up here one could see a lot of treetops, and several of their prospec-

4

tive neighbors' roofs. From this place, in mid-June, it seemed a hot, green land in which they dwelt. Of the great metropolis that sprawled around them not much was visible except for part of the highway that ran past a block to the east, the shopping center on the highway's other side, and the three towers looming over the horizon to mark the location of the central city.

This house would be wind-blasted in the winter (one reason Dan wanted to go up into the attic was to check the insulation) but the summer breezes were certainly pleasant, and the occupant would never have to worry about a flood, even in the wettest spring. The hill that the house stood on was perhaps the highest place in the generally flat terrain for a mile or more around.

The settler who had built this place had doubtless a wide choice of sites—and like many others of his time he had chosen high. At the time from which the house supposedly dated, well before the Civil War, the surrounding land must have been largely virgin prairie. Chicago, then far beyond and below the horizon to the east, would have been a small collection of frame buildings, a booming but otherwise unremarkable town, perhaps not yet incorporated as a city. From this window one neighboring farmhouse may have been visible, on the next mile-distant hill, and maybe not. Dan wondered if there had been a road. And Indians . . . in what year had the Black Hawk War been fought? He would ask Nancy sometime.

Now of course pavement was everywhere beneath the green suburban canopy of trees, and automobiles had managed to proliferate rapidly enough to keep the ever-extending acres of concrete and asphalt crowded. Not many sidewalks

around here, in the better suburban neighborhoods' best tradition. Main Street, a principal
thoroughfare of Wheatfield Park and also a num-
bered state highway, ran north and south one
block to the east of the old house Nancy and Dan
were looking at. The house itself faced south, its
irregular half-acre lot fronting on Benham Road,
which cut west from Main to lose itself a few
blocks farther west in residential meanders and
cul de sacs. As Ventris had already pointed out,
Benham at no time of day sustained a very heavy
flow of traffic, and the kids would not be running
out of their yard directly into a busy highway.
They were still young enough for that to be important.

Across Benham, the land sloped downhill into
the large backyards of the next street's houses. To
the east on Benham, the nearest house was a contemporary four-bedroom-sized brick ranch; Dan
was looking down now upon its elegant tile roof.
On the next lot to the west stood a green-vinyl-
sided Georgian, with a wide immaculate lawn and
a well-manicured flower garden in the back; the
back yard of the house beyond that was graced by
a large in-ground swimming pool. The house on
the hilltop had the look of a poor relation amid
its much newer neighbors.

Not that it was a ruin, or seemed abandoned. It
had been vacant, according to Ventris, for only a
few weeks. "Rundown" was not exactly the right
word, either; the white stucco that now covered
the outside walls seemed reasonably solid, and
there were no other obvious signs of deteriora-
tion. The plumbing, as Dan had already satisfied
himself, was in working condition, and the wiring
was modern enough. Standing now on the folding

chair that Ventris had finally unearthed from the back of a closet, and thrusting his head up through an obviously little-used trapdoor into the dimness of the attic, Dan saw nothing horrifying. It was hot, of course, though louvered vents in opposite gables allowed air circulation as well as admitting a little light. But there was no sign of leaks in the roof. The ancient wooden beams and joists looked hand-hewn, and the nearest of them felt as solid as a young oak when Dan jabbed at it with the smallest and sharpest blade of his little pocket-knife. The attic was largely unfloored, but there was at least some kind of insulation between the joists.

He would check it out more thoroughly, later, if they really got serious about the place. "Looks dry, at least," he said, getting down off the chair and brushing the dust of decades from his hands. He looked at Nancy, trying to gauge what she was really feeling about the place, and saw his own thoughtful uncertainty mirrored in her face; they could take another turn around, but essentially they had seen it all now, from top to bottom.

Ventris was being unobtrusive in the background, and the children were rapping on a bedroom wall in quest of hollow places that might have been used as hidey-holes for escaping slaves. "I would say the owners have tried to keep it up," Dan offered, probing for his woman's opinion.

Nancy shook her head and frowned. "I would say they've tried too hard."

That was it, Dan thought. The owners down through the years, or at least some of the most recent of them, had seemingly worked on the place too much, and too often at cross purposes. It was no longer apparent to the casual eye that the house, or a large part of it at least, might date from well before the Civil War. It had been added to, sided, remodeled, stuccoed, re-sided, re-remodeled, re-stuccoed, modernized and remodernized until even its original outlines had disappeared and it was hard to tell where the original walls stood, or of what they had been made.

Someone with more imagination and energy than talent, doubtless the present owner or an ambitious do-it-yourselfer in his family, had recently completed the latest assault. This had been sustained mainly by the kitchen and the downstairs bath. Besides the refrigerator and regular stove, which were to stay, an off-brand oven had been built into the kitchen wall at shoulder height, surrounded by panels of unconvincing brick and stone whose corners were already starting to peel back from the wall. What appeared to be a new window in the downstairs bath would not close quite all the way, and the fancy new medicine cabinet wiggled like a loose tooth in its socket when you slid the mirrored door open, and dribbled a little plaster dust from around its edges. Also downstairs, in the living room, a real fireplace had at some time had its flue bricked up and been made to look artificial. And then there was the way the one-car frame garage clung to the side of the house, almost like a lean-to glued on with filets of siding and stucco. No door led directly from house to garage, though there were four (count 'em four) doors leading from the ground floor to outside. Every kind of wall covering ever devised by the mind of man seemed to be findable somewhere on the interior walls in at least one of the multiplicity of rooms. All in all, as Nancy had protested, a real hodgepodge.

And yet—and yet. On the plus side, there was all that room, the four bedrooms for a family perhaps to be enlarged, since Nancy had said she wanted a baby of her own. There was the basic structural soundness, the fireplace to resurrect when time and money permitted, the tall old windows with their ancient glass. And who knew what buried glories or original woodwork, floors, and paneling were waiting to be uncovered? Besides the house itself there was the external space that came with it, a vast irregular plot of lawn or rather yard, that showed permanent-looking worn spots in the form of a children's impromptu softball diamond, and was otherwise mostly luxuriant crabgrass somewhat in need of mowing. No well-kept garden like the neighbors', but plenty of room for kids to play and things to grow. One might plant vegetables here, or keep a dog, or both.

They looked into each bedroom once more, then went downstairs and walked through all the ground floor rooms again. When they finally stood outside, with Ventris locking the place up, Nancy stood frowning up at the old place in a way that had nothing to do with the bright sun in her eyes. "It's a hodgepodge," she repeated.

"It sure is," Dan agreed. But then, instead of herding the children right back to Ventris' car, the two of them continued gazing at the place, as they might have looked at some objectionable relative with whom they had been stuck by fate and who therefore had to be gotten on with at almost any cost. The children meanwhile were making themselves right at home in the yard, arguing about where the exact highest point of the hilltop was. They were both wrong, it was right under the house. Sometimes Dan wondered if they were really as bright as their teachers had sometimes indicated.

"They're only asking sixty-two five," Dan said to himself, meditating aloud. And then he kicked himself mentally for that *only*, which Ventris could not have failed to hear.

"I would say it's no great bargain," Nancy commented, giving her fiancee a sharp look. "Children, I think that's supposed to be some kind of flowerbed near the porch, please stay out of it." She was easing into the Mother role somewhat ahead of time, with Dan's full approval.

"Well, I suppose there are two schools of thought about that," said Ventris, standing patiently beside them now. "The house itself is not the prettiest or the most convenient, but those things can always be changed. The land itself, in this area . . ."

Allowing himself to be tugged along by the soft sell, Dan knew a growing feeling of *rightness* about the place. The taxes were reasonable, at least in terms of suburban taxes in general, good schools were supposedly nearby (that was another thing to be checked out more closely), and he had a theory that it was better to own the cheapest house on the block, any block, rather than the best. Let your neighbors' property pull the value of your own property up, not down. And after a couple of days of house-looking he had seen enough to realize that he was not going to be able to afford, for example, that four-bedroom brick ranch next door.

"Do you think the owners might come down a little bit?" Nancy was asking the agent. "If we *should* decide to buy this place, it would take quite a bit of money to fix it over to what we want." Dan had earlier suffered occasional pangs of private fear that an offwhite wife with eyes adorned by a trace of epicanthic folds might be made to feel unwelcome in suburbia, where folk of Oriental descent seemed almost as rare as blacks or poverty. So far no problems, though, not even a funny look, at least as far as Dan had been able to observe. And, by judging by Nancy's demeanor, the idea that there might be racial problems for her had never entered her head.

Ventris compressed his lips and answered her cautiously. "I'm not sure. I rather suspect they *might* be open to an offer, though the price is already low for this area. Did I mention before that the family has been having personal problems?"

"No, you didn't," said Nancy. "Nervous breakdowns, I suppose, from the look of that remodeling in the kitchen."

"Something like that. The man of the house suffered some kind of breakdown, and then he did away with himself."

"Oh, I'm sorry." She really was. "I was trying to be funny, in my own stupid way. I didn't have any idea."

"Come on, kids, let's get in the car," Dan called. To Ventris he said: "We're going to have to think about this place."

"Maybe the joint is haunted," Dan commented a minute later, without really knowing why, looking back at the vacant and intriguing house one more time before he got into the car and closed the door.

Ventris just shook his head and gave a little laugh. "That's one thing I haven't heard anybody say."

11

. CHAPTER .

2

By the time he pulled the rented van off Benham Road Dan had gotten pretty well used to driving it. He backed up into his yard—his yard!—with some dexterity, minimizing the carrying distance between truck and house.

Nancy's Volkswagen was in the small garage, whose doors she had managed to prop open with some bricks. Nancy herself, in jeans and with a kerchief tied round her head, was standing in the shade-mottled yard, talking with a stoutish lady in gardening clothes.

Nancy's brother Larry, chunky in his junior college sweatshirt, called out to her from the van to get to work; then Larry and Dan's friend Howie, who had been following in Dan's Plymouth, got the rear door of the van open and immediately began to struggle to get some of Dan's furniture unloaded. Nancy's father Ben, who had kept Dan and Larry entertained with Navy stories all the way out from the city, got out of the right seat beside Dan and went to pitch right in.

Millie and Sam, who had ridden out with Nancy earlier, now came running from the backyard to get under the movers' feet and be yelled at, and Dan, as soon as he had the chance, went to check in with Nancy. Her companion proved to be Mrs. Follett, their next-door neighbor to the west, of the vinylsided Georgian with all the flowers. Mrs. Follett had at first glance a plump look that Dan considered natural for a suburban matron at the end of middle age, but then you noticed her hands, which were shamelessly hardened by outdoor work, and a certain weathered toughness in her face that made her smile somehow much more attractive.

He would have to forgive poor Nancy here for not doing any other work, Mrs. Follett said, because getting to know the neighbors was a big part of the job of moving in. "Yes, and I've also introduced myself to Millie and Sam already. They're going to have a fine big yard to play in here, and Patrick and I won't mind a bit if they chase a ball or something over into our grass from time to time. I think fences are rather ugly. Don't set up your baseball diamond on my side of the line, is all I asked them." The unfenced property line was certainly plain enough, with rude crabgrass and dandelions on one side, prim civilized lawn in a meek carpet on the other. "And do try to stay out of the flowers!" This last was sent in a slightly raised voice toward the children, who were just coming out of the house again in a race to see who could carry some prize in from the van. They glanced over as if they might have heard the warning with at least half an ear. "The poor Stanton children. I bawled them out sometimes and now I'm sorry for it. Little did I know what trouble they were having in their family ... I suppose you've heard something of that."

Dan and Nancy exchanged glances. Nancy said: "We only saw Mrs. Stanton once, and very briefly. In the lawyer's office, when we were closing on the house."

"Well, he put an end to his own life." Mrs. Follett looked hard toward the old house for a moment, but then away again. "After a brief period of mental disturbance. But let's not dwell on the unhappiness of the past. You're getting a fine piece of property. You can be very happy with it—now look at those clouds. I hope it doesn't start to rain before you can get your furniture inside."

A mass of gray-white cumulonimbus blowing over from the southwest had passed the zenith and now shadowed Wheatfield Park, and grumbled threats at the poor creatures on the ground, who for the most part no doubt took calmly their situation beneath those kilotons of water. I wonder what room he did it in, Dan thought, turning away and walking over to help the other men unload his furniture. And how? Gunshot? A couple of the rooms had been repainted very recently. But no, he didn't really want to know.

The unloading and carrying everything in was, not surprisingly, just as big a job as loading had been. Despite all the stuff he had sold or given away before moving, the truck's cargo seemed remarkably vast to be only the belongings of one small family. And Nancy's stuff wasn't even included, of course. Her things would come later, when she moved out of her apartment in the city just before the wedding, which was to be in mid-August. Dan was taking a week of vacation starting now, from his engineering job in a Chicago architect's office, to get himself and the kids settled in here. He would take another later for a quick honeymoon while the kids spent a week in camp; then they would all settle in here as a family shortly before Labor Day, after which the youngsters would have to get started in their new school. It had been, and was, and would be, a hectic summer, and so far the days and weeks of it had flown by with almost bewildering speed.

The truck was unloaded before the rain began. Nancy meanwhile had taken the Volks to get a bag of hamburgers from a nearby drive-in. When she got back, it fell to Dan to walk over to the Folletts' and tell Nancy's father that lunch was ready. Mr. Patrick Follett, a graying and wiry retiree with steel-rimmed glasses, had dropped over to say hello and hit it off at once with Ben, to whom he was now demonstrating his automatic lawn sprinkling system. Mrs. Follett answered Dan's tap at their French doors with evident relief; she appeared to have some genuine fear of what the neighbors might think and say should they see the sprinklers operating in the rain.

When all the laborers had been refreshed with food and cooling drink, Larry and Howie and Ben boarded the truck to return it to the rental service in the city, and the Post family, including Nancy, got back to work. Dan, headed for the second floor with an armload of his clothes that had somehow been left misplaced in the kitchen and were blocking operations there, had just taken the first two ascending steps and turned on the low landing when the smell hit him. It was an odd, powerful

15

odor, that reminded him of rancid grease. The impact was so strong and sudden that he stopped in his tracks and turned around, trying to get a bearing on the source. But he had time for only a couple of sniffs before the smell faded away as fast as it had come.

When he had finished stowing the clothes upstairs, in the closet of what he now thought of as the master bedroom, and had come down again bringing some lamps that had earlier been taken up by mistake, he mentioned the smell to Nancy.

She was laboring in the kitchen, sorting pots and pans and non-perishable food items from moving boxes into the freshly washed cabinets. "I noticed a smell earlier. Sort of fishy and rotten."

"This wasn't fishy, exactly. It couldn't have been those drive-in hamburgers, could it? I hope we didn't poison anybody."

She shook her head. "I ate one and it seemed no worse than usual."

"Yeah, me too."

"I noticed the smell when I was carrying things down into the basement. I wish you'd go down and check those drains sometime soon."

"All right, I'll take a look," he agreed, humoring his bride. It was not the first time she had voiced suspicion of the drains, and Dan had come to realize that Ben's attitude toward basements, one of keeping a very taut ship with regard to pipes and drains and waterproofing, had left its mark upon his daughter. "Though I don't think we're likely to have any of that sort of trouble, up on a hill like this."

Shortly, loaded with another armful of miscellany (on moving day, no one goes anywhere emptyhanded), he went down into the basement. It was true that he had neglected to look at the drains, and he supposed that a trap could be plugged up, or some such thing. There never seemed to be enough time these days to do everything that had to be done, and his previous time in the basement had been spent mainly in checking out the old hot-water heating system as best he could, and in deciding where his wine cellar—that is, a couple of plastic racks for wine bottles—would best be located.

He flicked the light on as he came down now. The day had turned dark with the rain and the basement windows were small and blocked by shrubbery.

The whole basement, which extended under less than the whole area of the house above, was floored with smooth and reasonably new concrete, but the walls were a different story. In one section they were as modern as the floor, but elsewhere they were of yellow Illinois limestone. Dan stacked his miscellany against an unoccupied section of the wall and crouched there for a moment staring at its masonry. Comparing them to certain old buildings only a few score miles away where he had grown up, he would guess that these limestone walls might have been set in place sometime before the turn of the century. He sniffed over the nearest floor drain, sniffed again, then felt around for dampness in the shadowed corner; he could detect nothing but dust. Thunder grumbled outside. The past two days had been quite rainy but the whole basement looked perfectly dry. It was also cleaner than he had expected.

From where he stood now in the shadowed corner he could see behind the furnace, and there, just as he had noticed them when making his in-

17

spection of the heating system, were a new sledge-hammer and a wrecking bar. The tools looked unused, and he had made a mental note on discovering them to find out who they belonged to and hand them over—and then had promptly forgotten his mental note in the press of other business. Now it looked as if they were going to be his, though it didn't seem that they were likely to be of any immediate use.

As he looked behind the furnace along the limestone wall his attention was caught by the wall that it met farther on; this cross-wall was like nothing he had seen in a house before. Earlier he had had no time to pay it more attention than a brief check for dryness and solidity. Now he walked around the furnace for a closer examination.

This was the basement's oldest-looking wall, and extended the width of the house, which beyond this wall had only a low crawl space beneath it. The wall was made of smooth, round stones, such as might have been picked up from a creek- or river-bed somewhere. The stones were mostly about fist-size, cemented together with solid-looking mortar. Dan scraped at a mortar joint with a finger, and a single particle the size of a sand grain came off. All dry as dust. No evil smells. Dan took a final look around and then went up the stairs and back to work.

On that Saturday night, his first night in the old house, Dan experienced for the first time what he later came to think of as an Indian dream. On this first night the dream began with him, or rather with some stranger's body in which he had inexplicably come to dwell, striding across a seemingly endless prairie. He was surrounded by grass the color of golden toast, which in places grew higher than his head. Dan was completely without influence over the movements of his (or rather the stranger's) body in the dream, which was extraordinarily vivid and self-consistent, at least in its earlier part. Whether because this peculiar vividness gave the dream a semblance of reality, or for some other reason, the anxiety of incipient nightmare was building and had been from the start, though he knew he was asleep, and so far the dream had recounted nothing horrible.

The eyes of his dream-self turned down briefly and frequently to gauge the footing of the uneven ground beneath the trackless grass. The first time it happened Dan had observed with some surprise that the body he inhabited was brown-skinned, hairlessly smooth, and almost entirely naked. He wore moccasins, and a small loincloth of some rough fabric. Around his neck an amulet or ornament of shell swung on a fragile-looking string of grass. His bare brown chest and wiry arms were painted with stripes and circles of white and ocher. In its right hand the dream-body carried a small box or cup that seemed to have been made by folding some material that looked and felt like smooth treebark. The fingers that held the cup were thin and dark, and the whole body was taut with sharply delineated muscle. The smell of rancid grease was in the air.

Dan had been inhabiting the body, in a state of surprise and mounting anxiety, for some six or eight of its strides before he interpreted certain steadily recurrent sounds as being made by the feet of at least two other people walking with him, keeping just behind him and to each side, as if

19

they were either giving a formal escort or perhaps guarding him as a prisoner. The sounds were evidently familiar to the man whose body he tenanted; the body did not turn its head to see who followed. Though he was looking through its eyes, Dan could not alter the direction of the body's gaze by so much as a fraction of a millimeter.

The dream-body raised its arms and Dan felt the light scratching of glass blades across them as it pushed through a screen of grass somewhat taller than most of the field, and now with this obstacle past a somehow familiar hill was plainly visible. At the same time there came into his view a distant line of bent and brown-skinned toilers, a file of laboring people that began somewhere far off on the grassy plain to his right and extended up the entire slope of the grass-covered hill ahead, to a new mound of bare grayish earth that crowned its top. The line of workers a hundred yards or so ahead was part of an endless chain of men and women wearing loincloths and little else. They ascended the hill under the weight of large wicker baskets that appeared to be overflowing with earth, each basket held on its bearer's bent back by a tumpline going round the forehead. Another line of workers came steadily downhill at an easy pace, walking tall with baskets empty, going back off to the right across the prairie.

Around the top of the hill there hung a small cloud of dry dust, floating against a lightly overcast sky. Besides the carriers bringing up earth, other men and women were at work up there, toiling and tamping with what seemed to be hoes and mauls and shovels in their hands. One in a feathered headdress seemed to be giving orders. The distance was still too great for Dan to observe the work in detail. But he was being taken closer.

Dan had plenty of time to think about his experience even as it was happening, and he understood that it was some kind of dream. Yet he did not wake up, and his sense of anxiety increased somewhat. The body in which he dwelt continued to advance with steady paces that shortened somewhat as it began to climb the hill. The feet that walked behind him and to his sides maintained their own steady sounds and relative positions.

Together the walkers went on up the hill, Dan's baseless fear increasing as they climbed. He had the feeling that it might be his host's fear as well as his own. The eyes through which he saw remained fixed directly ahead, toward the work proceeding on the hilltop. Now he saw that another crew was busy there, a little to one side of those heaping earth. The second group of laborers, fewer in number, had erected a framework of freshly cut and trimmed logs; it was like a giant picture frame with nothing in it.

As Dan and his escort neared the top of the hill, the nature of the construction there became more readily observable. Basically it was the piling up of a tremendous mound of earth, in successive hard-packed layers. A narrow, bending passageway open at the top led into the mound between high, straight earthen walls. Atop the walls a score of workers were raking and stamping and pounding down the dirt as quickly as the slow but endless chain of bearers could dump the contents of their baskets out. Others added water to the dirt, enough to give it some cohesion without making mud. The picture-frame of logs stood isolated to one side, and although the corner of his host's vision brought Dan the view of some people moving about there, he could not see what they were doing. All around the top of the hill the grass had been worn away by human feet.

Dan would have described the people around him, including his host, as American Indians, though of what time or tribe he could not have begun to guess. At his host's approach workers ceased working, and they and their overseer in the feathered headdress stepped back deferentially when they found they were in his path. Several men spoke to Dan's host, most of them repeating the same words, in a language totally unfamiliar to Dan. Each was given the same reply.

His host's path led toward the opening in the mound, to the narrow gateway that led in through raw earthen walls, to . . . to what could not yet be seen. Just as it reached the gateway his host body stopped, and raised the cup it carried in what was evidently a ritual gesture. At the same time it faced around, and Dan could for the first time see those who had come walking through the tall grass with him and up the hill. They were a pair of young men painted as Dan somehow knew his host was. Each carried a bark bucket larger than his, and their eyes like all others' were on Dan's host as he, the medicine man, held up his bark cup toward the sun and chanted loud words meaningless to Dan.

When the shaman lowered his eyes again and looked about him at his world, Dan got his first good look at the country round the hill. Here and there were small groves of trees Dan could recognize as white pines, and what appeared to be some kind of autumn-foliaged oaks. The ocean of tall grass, spotted with such groves and clumps of trees, stretched out to the rolling horizon. Now Dan marked how the long line of bearers that wound down from the hill traversed perhaps half a mile of prairie to another hillock from which dry earth was evidently being dug. Somewhat closer, and in the direction from which the body he inhabited had just walked, a village lay near a tree-marked watercourse, a collection of round-topped huts with people moving about them. It was a wilderness, a world almost unmarked by man except for the one small village and the few footpaths about the hill and the earthen construction rising up its top.

Dan's host now spoke briefly to his people once again. And then he turned, slowly, as if reluctant to face what must now be faced atop the hill, inside the walls of earth on which his people labored so. Not walls, perhaps, at all, but more accurately a monolith or pyramid of rammed earth through which a single roofless passage had been left.

The fear was certainly the dream-body's now, as well as Dan's, for now the wiry arms and legs were quivering with it. But despite his fear, and with his trembling assistants now following perforce in single file, the shaman entered the passageway that led into the mass of compacted earth. The passageway was not long, but twice turned at right angles.

In an open space in the center of the earthwork a pit several yards deep—Dan could not see exactly how deep it was—had been dug down below the natural top of the hill. Resting partially in this pit, with the new, massive walls of tamped earth rising closely about its upper portion on all sides

23

so there was hardly room for the narrow ledge where the shaman and his two assistants stood, was a tower as big as a farmer's silo, shaped roughly like a bottle with a slightly tapered neck. The tapered upper end of the bottle was several feet below the earthworks' top, and whatever details of feature might have marked its solid surface were concealed beneath a perpetual glaze of unearthly-looking fire. The film of flame was so blue as to be nearly ultraviolet, on the dim edge of the visible spectrum. It clung as closely to the tower as a film of water, and within the film the purls of bluish flame were in ceaseless, random-seeming flow. Standing almost within arm's length of the blue fire, the shaman's body felt only the faintest glow of heat.

As soon as the three men had arrived within the earth enclosure, there came a heavy click from inside the tower. A section of blue flame the size of a small door, at a level a little above their eyes, somehow detached itself and folded inward, leaving a lightless doorway where it had been. The chief medicineman raised his eyes, and raised the bark vessel in his trembling right hand as if in offering, and inside the newly opened doorway his eyes caught a swift movement of something that appeared large as a man but was inhuman and dull gray.

The continuity of the dream broke then for the first time, and in the next moment Dan was watching (through whose eyes he did not know) a young woman or teenaged girl with long, ornamented Indian hair, her body stripped and painted in two colors, left and right. She was being tied by her hands and feet to the giant picture frame of logs, as cloth might be secured during its weaving, or a hide that was going to be stretched. Around Dan bows were being bent, and as the stone-tipped arrows were drawn to their full length against the curving wood the terror of the dream mounted to new heights, and now as if in mercy the vision became more truly dream-like, began to be jumbled and incoherent.

For the first time Dan could now move his point of vision at will, and he turned in horror from the sacrifice and looked down the hill's long slope of golden grass to mark how the shopping center sprang into existence in the meadow below. And now the charging automobiles of Main Street's morning commuter rush roared four abreast, like racing chariots, around the base of the hill, and headed up a dry creek bed which they filled from bank to bank.

Dan was clothed now in a business suit, heading for the office with vast relief, and in his hand he carried a briefcase instead of a bark cup filled with stinking lard. As he strode down the hill to go to work, from the old frame house behind him there came the sound of a piano badly in need of tuning, picking out some old old melody he should have recognized. He looked around and saw his dead wife playing, but instead of being in a coffin or a hospital bed she was sitting up in a strange container of glassy plastic, and he awoke with a last gasp of fear.

. CHAPTER .

3

In the business of supervising the children's
choice of clothes and preparing breakfast on a
rainy Sunday morning he started to forget his
dream; when he routinely asked the children how
their first night in the house had been, they
claimed to have slept well, but Dan recalled hearing them toss restlessly during the night, and he
had gone to look in on Sammy once after the boy
cried out in his sleep. That had been before his
own crazy Indian dream of moundbuilding and
flaming giant bottles and sacrifice. Even though
he had started to forget his own dream, it
wouldn't die. It persisted in the back of his mind
as something indigestible might lie ominously in
the stomach.

At breakfast, the kids wondered how Mrs.
Wright, their Chicago housekeeper, was doing.

"Maybe it's my cooking that makes you yearn

for her. Well, a few more weeks of my efforts and then Nancy will be taking over."

Millie asked: "Is she a good cook?"

"She will be. We'll give her lots of chances to practice."

Nancy arrived on schedule, in the heat of noon, to continue to work on the cleaning and fixing up and settling in. "Zap," she said, when Sam opened the front door for her, and shot him neatly in the chest with a small but evidently powerful water pistol. He screamed with joy, and Millie came running to get in on the fun. Nancy naturally had brought a weapon for each of them.

"Everyone sleep well?" she asked Dan brightly after they had kissed and greeted.

"Fairly well, I guess." He told her about the dream in some detail, trying to cleanse his mind of it.

After lunch the kids went out on the porch to play and the adults got to work. Dan was washing down a wall in the living room when Nancy called him upstairs to tell him about a woodsmoke smell. "I just caught a whiff of it, and now it's gone."

Smoke was considerably more alarming than old grease, and he went on an immediate investigation—basement, ground floor, upstairs rooms. No smoke.

Then he decided to check the attic. He got a chair and pushed open the door in the hall ceiling and climbed up, this time armed with a flashlight, to poke again with his knife at the old timbers. The air smelled vaguely damp, which was only natural considering all the rain they had been getting recently. More was thrumming now, with its curiously soothing sound, upon the roof. No smell of smoke, though, or of rancid grease for that matter. Come to think of it, that grease smell had even permeated last night's dream.

Shining the light about, he saw with satisfaction that his roof was perfectly dry on the inside. But when he turned the light down on the ceiling joists, satisfaction faded. As he had noted in his earlier brief inspection, the spaces between the exposed joists had mostly been filled with insulating material. Looking more critically now, however, he realized that this insulation, like so much else about the house, was a patchwork of good and bad.

Only in small areas of the large attic were the sturdy old joists covered with anything like permanent flooring. In other places planks had been put down, loose, to walk on; otherwise moving about was a matter of tightrope walking on the joists, to keep from putting a foot and leg through soft insulation and the unprotected lath and plaster of the ceiling below. Dan could see now that in some areas the insulation was modern, rolls or batts of thick, vermin-proof, fireproof mineral fiber, doubtless underlain by a plastic vapor barrier. Alas, in other places the situation was different.

Switching on his flashlight, Dan began to poke around in the far corners, close under the angle of the roof. There he dug down and in between joists with his fingers, and came up with a handful of clotted granules that looked as old as the house itself. After a moment's distasteful puzzlement he realized with practical horror that someone had once poured in sawdust as insulation here. It was now gray and appeared to be dryly rotting; mixed in with his handful were what looked like coprolithic mouse droppings, and a discarded insect shell or two.

The tasks of washing walls and settling in downstairs could wait. Sawdust invited vermin and fire—Nancy's sniff of woodsmoke made him suspicious now of spontaneous combustion—and it was going to have to go. Today.

Dan descended into the house, and there in exasperation conferred with Nancy. After refusing lunch until later he went down into the basement, located his metal cutters and a usable tin can, and fashioned himself a serviceable sawdust scoop. It was still early afternoon when he was back in the attic, excavating its remoter areas.

Digging in a place where only fingers would fit, an almost inaccessible angle behind the ancient stone chimney that still went up from the sealed fireplace below, he suddenly found a solid object in his grasp. When he brought the thing out into the light, and brushed off the debris that clung to it, it proved to be a book. It was not much bigger than his hand, and its plain red cover looked unfaded and unworn.

The book opened in his fingers with a stiff little crackling sound; the binding was still firm and the pages were unyellowed. They were also for the most part blank, he saw with minor disappointment as he flipped through them from back to front. Not entirely blank, though; the first ten or twelve pages had been filled with small handwriting in dim blue ink. The writing was too thin and tiny, and its style was a little to different from what he was used to reading, for him to be able to make it out readily in the bad light. (The flashlight's batteries were pooping out, it seemed;

something else to buy.) But it seemed to be a diary of some kind. Was that date 1857? Or 1851?

A minute later he was down in the living room, smiling as he held out a little surprise present for Nancy, who had a frown on her face as she washed at the walls Dan had abandoned.

"Care for a little romance and excitement, honey?"

"I could use some about now." She looked with mock hopefulness at the book. "Sex manual?"

"Elevate your thoughts. I would say it's more like a genuine historical document." He described briefly how and where he had found the book.

She was impressed and delighted, and he suspected that she would have sat down at once to study it but for an outbreak of riotous noise from the children in the kitchen that sent her striding toward the scene like an experienced mother. Dan followed, hanging back a little with the purpose of letting her handle the disturbance and solidly backing up whatever verdict she handed down.

One water pistol had already been lost, and the pair were fighting over the other, Millie temporarily not at all too grown up to express a violent interest in such matters. Pausing to drop the book into her shoulder bag that hung on the back of a kitchen chair, Nancy confiscated the offending weapon, and tossed it on the counter beside the sink with the warning that the two of them had better shape up or she was going to cease to bring them anything. This triggered some angry remarks by Millie; some firm rejoinders by Dan were required before at least an outward peace was re-established, and Nancy began putting together a belated lunch.

After lunch Nancy drove the kids, seemingly

reconciled with her, to the local movie theater. Arriving back at the house, she met Dan coming down from the attic, a sweaty and disheveled Santa shouldering a plastic leaf disposal bag filled with defunct insulation. A couple of similar bags were already outside the kitchen door, awaiting Wednesday's garbage pickup.

As soon as he had deposited the third and last bag outdoors he came back into the kitchen, where Nancy was already starting to wash some dishes, and they enjoyed a kiss, the first leisurely one, it seemed, in a long, long time . . . she pulled away and became prudently businesslike.

"So, tomorrow your vacation starts. Do you think you can line up a temporary housekeeper for the week after?"

He sat down in a kitchen chair. "Looks like I may have to. I brought up the subject of day camp again last night, and neither of the little angels was very receptive to the idea. Anyway—yeah, I've about decided on a housekeeper anyway. Friend of mine gave me the phone number of this eighteen-year-old blond Swedish girl who's look-ing for a job. Deserving orphan, I understand."

"Uh-huh. I see. Maybe I'd better do the inter-viewing for you."

"Oh, I wouldn't want to put you to any extra trouble, honey." He put his arms round Nancy once again, then let go abruptly and looked about the room. "Gad."

"What is it?"

"That smell again. The grease. You mean to say you didn't get it this time?"

"No, I don't smell anything at the moment, ex-cept just a hint of hard-working man. Me with my woodsmoke and you with your grease. Maybe we're both hallucinating. Oh, Dan, I forgot to tell you. Mrs. Follett was over before lunch, while you were upstairs working. Just dropped in and handed me something she turned up sometime last year in her garden. She called it an Indian arrowhead, and said she thought the children might be interested. Then the rebellion came along, and I never showed it to them. Do you suppose Millie really hates me?"

"Of course not. Mrs. Follett seems like a nice old gal."

"It's in my bag—well, my hands are wet now, I'll show you later. It may be more interesting than she knows. Dan, you know how the hill we're on here is sort of in two parts—a long, gentle rise, and then a sort of smaller knob that sits on top." She paused and considered. "It's really not as distinct a thing as I make it sound, but if you take a careful look sometime, you'll see the topography."

"All right, I take the expert's word for it. But so what?"

"I'm no expert, just because I work in public relations at a museum. But you see, Mrs. Follett's garden is really on the lower, gentler slope, right next to the upper knob . . . well, never mind. I'd better get my facts straight and my theories organized before I bring them out into the open."

He moved a little closer. "Reveal them now. Or, if not your theories, something else." Eyes narrowing, he leered, forefinger stroking an imaginary mustache. "We are all alone, my child, in this secluded place. No one will be able to hear your screams, or come to your aid."

"The wedding is in about five weeks, buster. Right now I'm the suburban mother type, remember? No longer the single city swinger." She puffed a pure kiss at him from a safe distance and then primly turned her back. "All right, maybe I'd *better* keep talking about my archaeological theories. I'm sure our neighbor lady is right, and what she brought me is a projectile point, or what she calls an arrowhead, but it may be a little more exciting than just that. Let me check with the guys at the Museum."

"Fine, sure, I'm all in favor of science. Now how about some beer or lemonade, if I can't interest you in anything more sinister?"

"Well . . ."

On his second night in the old house, Dan Post dreamed what he later came to think of as the farm-boy dream. It began, as had the Indian dream, with him walking in a stranger's body, this time under a clear blue sky in the dull heat of summer. Open fields surrounded him again, but this time the grass was greener and not nearly so tall. Some hundreds of yards ahead, a curving line of trees marked out what must be a watercourse. Insects droned; the air smelled very soft and clean.

His host body was fully clothed this time, he saw through its occasionally downturned eyes, except for bare feet that were sunburned and dirty and tough-looking. Some kind of a broad hat was on his head, a lock of dark hair hung before his eyes, and he wore a shirt with long sleeves rolled up, and baggy trousers or overalls held up by a single cloth suspender. His shadow walked slightly ahead of him through trackless grass and clover, and another of about equal size slid along companionably beside it.

When Dan's host turned his head to the left Dan saw that the companion was a freckled, red-headed boy of perhaps eleven or twelve, almost exactly the same height as Dan's host, and similarly dressed. Red's hair was long under his straw hat, and a line of fragile down descended his cheek where whiskers would begin to sprout in a few years. Red was talking as the dream began, but in so alien a dialect that it took Dan a few moments to realize that the language was English.

". . . an' my Da says that ol' man Schwartz be crazy," were the first words that made sense to Dan.

"Reckon it's so?" the childish vocal cords of his dream-body answered, and as if prompted by the thought the head turned away to the right, and his gaze lifted over a field blooming with summer clover to behold, in the distance, the house on the hill. It was of weathered wood instead of white stucco, and it lacked a garage and seemed too tall and narrow. Now even the tall windows were the same, but yet Dan knew without thinking that this house stood on the same hill as that on which his own sleeping body lay. As on the previous night he understood that he was dreaming, but there was nothing he could do to rouse himself. He tried, for although there was no horror in this dream, not yet, the style and the clarity of it connected it with the terrible Indian dream of the night before.

The two boys walked on through the summer heat, conversing sporadically about the prospects of going to sea when they grew up. From what Dan could see, the countryside appeared to be little more settled than it had during the Indian dream, with only the one house now in sight. Several times the eyes of Dan's host turned in that direction, and once Dan saw a tall figure, as of a man in dark clothing, standing motionless in the yard. The figure was too far away for any detail to be visible, and by the time of the next glance back, a few moments later, it was gone.

Now less than a hundred yards ahead was the curving, tree-bordered line of the watercouse that wound between the gentle, unfenced hills. When the distance had grown a little smaller still, both boys began to run despite the heat.

"Peter, last one in's a rotten cowpie!" the red-head cried.

The young body Dan moved in ran and skipped, hopping limberly on first one foot and then the other as it shed its trousers without stopping. At last the muddy water ahead came into view, now very close. The wide straw hat went flying, and the rough shirt came off in a moment over the head. There were no undergarments to be bothered with. The stripping was finished just in time, as they reached the high bank above the brown surface of the stream. Really a small river, it was something like thirty feet wide at this point and evidently dependably deep even in summer. Red's white body flashed in a headfirst dive just ahead of him as Peter went off the bank in a broadjump. The sun-warm water smacked at them and took them in; Dan felt the soft mud bottom under Peter's feet, and soon found that the boy could stand no more than chin deep in the deepest part.

Red and Pete splashed and dog-paddled and floated and cooled themselves, and in a minute or two climbed out to sit bare-bottomed on a dead tree. Pale gray and barkless, the tree had fallen some time ago so as to nearly bridge the creek. The fallen tree, supported solidly only at one end, moved and dipped beneath the bathers' weight; it

35

would make a springier diving board than the bank.

Red began to discuss the feasibility of setting some kind of trap in here for turtles. Peter mostly listened. After a while there was a faint noise from upstream, back in the brush that lined the bank on the side toward the Schwartz house, that was visible still on its far hilltop, the bank opposite that from which the boys had jumped. Dan would doubtless have ignored the noise, but Peter and Red were both instantly alerted by it. Talk ceased. For a time all was quiet, save for a drone of insects somewhere near.

"Injuns!" whispered Peter at last, grinning, doubtless trying to be funny.

"Ain't no Injuns closer'n the Rock River." Red's tone was contemptuous, but almost equally quiet. He turned away from the direction of the noise, but as soon as the faint sound came again, perhaps a little closer, he turned right back. Something about it bothered these woods-wise kids.

"Maybe it's a b'ar, then." Peter joked, but he was listening carefully, too.

"Ol' caow o' Schwartz's, more'n likely." Red got up to a one-knee crouch on the log, and then stood, hanging on to a dead branch with each hand to help his balance. Pete squatted, bare toes gripping the tree bole. Red, peering intently off into the thick-leaved bushes, murmured: "Now, there's *somethin'* . . ."

It burst out of the bushes in a sudden charge toward them, no cow nor bear nor Indian. Though big enough to be a man, it was built low to the ground, no higher than a dog, and was inhuman and dull gray. Through Peter's momentarily frozen eyes Dan saw with merciless clarity that it moved on six legs instead of four, and that its feet were sheep-like hooves. Hairless and faceless and seemingly even without a head, it lunged toward the boys as fast as any animal might pounce.

Red, hemmed in on the log by branches, sprang from it in the only direction clearly open to him, landed on the same muddy bank the creature occupied, and ran. Peter's thoughtless instinct took him in the opposite direction, with a single leap into the water. Choking, lashing out awkwardly, he swam with scrambling fear-maddened strokes for the far bank. There two more seconds of nightmarish climbing brought him to its top.

From the top of the high bank he took one glance back over his shoulder. Red lay on his belly on the far bank, open-eyed but still as death. He had not been able to run far. From between his shoulder blades there protruded something that glinted in the sun, something that looked like a fine needle long as a man's hand. The mud-colored, monstrous creature, looking vaguely like a giant crab with six hoofed feet, had already turned its attention from Red and was coming after Peter. It had started out to cross the stream on the fallen log, which sank low beneath its heaviness. It clung there on the swaying log, hanging on with six legs and several tentacles or arms, and it had no face . . .

With a terror that was as much Dan's as his own, Peter turned and fled, knowing that his legs could not run fast enough to get away if Red's had not, knowing that he was going to be caught . . .

▪ CHAPTER ▪

4

On Monday his farm-boy dream of the night before stayed with him even more clearly than the Indian dream had done, and more depressingly as well. Maybe the headshrinkers whose popularizations he had occasionally sampled were right, maybe things from your childhood came back in strange disguises to clobber you when your adult self was laboring under stress and strain. Getting married, even to Nancy, meant stress and strain, all right, and so did selling one house and buying another one and getting moved.

Not that his childhood memories included a scene even remotely like that one. But maybe such a scene existed and he had blanked it out. No, that was nonsense. Well, what the hell, he was still sane and functioning. Right now he had more important things to do than nurse his psyche, such as caring for his extant family and getting his house in shape for his new bride.

Endless things to do. On Monday morning the telephone man came, and Dan felt back in communication with the world again. He unpacked and stowed and fixed up. What was he going to do about that wobbly medicine chest in the wall of the downstairs bath? Seemed like a comparatively simple problem but he wasn't sure how to go about solving it.

For lunch he and the kids had peanut butter sandwiches—Sam had recently taken to wanting his with raw onions and/or sliced bananas—and then they all went on a small shopping trip, and got some cash out of his new account at the local bank. Home again to do a little more work, and pretty soon it was time for dinner. Dan fried some hamburgers—again—and opened a couple of cans of peas. Well, if the kids kept eating it, he could keep on dishing it out.

Right after dinner, at the arranged time, he gave his love a call on the new phone. "Hi, baby."

"Hi, Dan. Listen, I don't think I'm going to be able to drive out tonight. Do you mind very much? I had quite a day on the job, and I'm dead tired."

"S'all right, Nan, I wasn't even expecting you tonight, remember? Take care of yourself. We're coping here."

"Good. Listen, Dan, you know the projectile point? I was right."

"Projectile point. Oh, yeah."

"It's what the guys at the Museum call a Helton point, or a Matanzas side-notched point. Similar ones have been found at the Koster site, and elsewhere in southern Illinois. Never right around here. They're thought to be around five thousand years old." The tiredness in Nancy's voice was giving way to animation as she talked. "One doesn't just turn them up in one's garden, as a rule."

"Well, that's great, I guess. I suppose it means eventually we'll have Museum people out here digging up our yard."

"The thought *had* just barely crossed my mind, but I wasn't sure how you'd react."

"Tremendous." His voice was somewhat dry, but he had to smile. "What about the book?"

"Oh, that." Nancy's voice became more thoughtful. "Well, it's—*weird*. You're definitely not the hoaxing type, or I'd certainly be suspicious. Come on, though, you read the book through before you gave it to me. You were pulling my leg about the greasy smell, and the dream."

"Pulling your leg? That's a nice thought. But no, I wasn't. And hey, I didn't tell you yet about the dream I had last night." And he proceeded to do so, or he tried. He suspected that over the phone it sounded no more impressive or remarkable than any other particularly vivid dream. But it and the Indian dream had both been—something apart from ordinary experience. Trying to convey that, though, was hard and made him feel a little silly.

"Oh, Dan. Sometimes I worry about you." Nancy sounded about half serious. "I wish I was out there already, looking after you. And how are the kids, still sleeping well?"

"They're fine. Well, if you're really worried about me, rush on out. We'll find a place for you to sleep—somewhere. Heh, heh."

"Mmm-hmm. Sure. I just better not find any blond housekeepers when I do arrive. Oh, damn, did I say I'd come out tomorrow night? That's

Tuesday evening, the shower, how could I have forgotten that? Oh, Danny."

They went on to calculate that she would come out on Wednesday evening, or in the afternoon if she could get away from work a little early. The conversation went on to Museum shoptalk, and to other topics after that.

On Monday night, Dan's third night in the old house, there came the black-girl dream. As it started, he was standing in dark night and freezing cold, helping someone else who seemed to be carrying a burden in one arm to get down from the flat bed of some kind of truck or wagon.

Overhead there stretched a sprawl of stars, unbelievably numerous and bright. There was no moon. Ice in a frozen puddle cracked under the shoes of Dan's new host body as it moved. It took him only a moment to realize that he had landed in a woman's body this time out; he could feel the unfamiliar bulge and weight of two full breasts as he reached his arms up to help another woman climb down from the rear of the wagon. From amidst a dim load of what looked like canvas stretched over straw the second woman came, the brilliant starlight letting Dan see her well enough to tell that she was a black girl who carried a baby-sized bundle held close against her with one arm. Behind her a young black man in dark, rough clothes also came crawling from concealment on the wagon. In a moment the two women and the man were standing in a huddle of unforced intimacy against the cold, the baby held more or less sheltered among their bodies.

Someone else, a little distance off, murmured something in a low voice, and the wagon began to roll away, hard-rimmed wheels going with a thud and rumble over frozen ruts. From beyond the piled-up load there came the clop of horses' feet and the mutter of their breath as the wagon moved.

Wordlessly, the black man who stood with the two women raised an arm, pointing up into the sky at an angle about halfway between the horizon and the zenith. The women lifted their faces to the sky.

It briefly crossed Dan's mind that he must be on some high mountaintop, such was the clarity of the stars. But this sky might never have known the smoke of automobiles and factories, and was certainly innocent of the electric glare of the cities that Dan knew. There was the familiar Dipper in the north, right side up for holding water; from the corner of the woman's vision Dan could see Polaris marking the pole almost exactly, but the eyes through which he saw were satisfied to find the Dipper and stay fixed on it for a long moment, while the woman let her lungs drink deep of icy air. Then she lowered her gaze and looked around.

They were standing atop a hill, but it was not a mountain. Even in the night Dan had no doubt of what hilltop he stood upon, though the house toward which the woman now turned her eyes was not objectively identifiable as his own. He got the impression that it was bigger than the tall house of the farm-boy dream. Only its dim outline could be seen lighted from within by what was probably the glow of a single lamp. No other light was visible in all the dark countryside around.

"In the house, in the house," a man's voice was urging now, coming from that direction, speaking English with a soft and somehow rural-sounding accent, though not one as hard for Dan to understand as Red's and Pete's had been.

Obediently the people from the wagon moved. Beckoning them on from a position near the door of the house was the man who evidently had just spoken. As the three came toward him Dan saw that this man was white, and quite tall, at least in comparison with the three blacks. The white man smiled at them encouragingly, and beckoned. He had rather close-set eyes, and a jutting chin that was further exaggerated by a small tuft of ginger beard. In the lamplight from a window he appeared to be in his forties, and was armored against the cold by a thick coat and a fur cap.

There in the farmyard just before the door of the house they were joined by another, shorter, white man, who came on foot from the direction of some dimly visible outbuildings, where he seemed to have just driven the wagon.

" 'Pears to me no one's likely to be about, Brother Clareson," this second white man said, swinging his arms and stamping his feet. "Reckon our gent'man passenger can he'p me with the horses iffn he's a mind to."

"Yassuh, yassuh, I do that." And the young black man accompanied the wagon driver back into the outer darkness, where the horses could be heard stamping in the cold.

"Hurry in then, Brother Hollister," the taller white called after them, low-voiced. "And we'll have some coffee for you both."

In the kitchen a white woman of the tall man's age or more was waiting for them, smiling with faded blue eyes and compressed lips. She was wearing a cheerfully patterned shawl about her shoulders, and had just set down a glasschimneyed lamp on a plain, scrubbed wooden table. On the wide top of a black metal kitchen stove, an enameled coffeepot sent up a breath of steam. The white woman, saying little but continuing to smile in a gentle, nearsighted way, began to hand out slabs of some kind of freshly baked cake, on small thick china plates.

The tall man called Clareson and the woman who was his wife or perhaps sister both urged the two black girls to take chairs at the scrubbed wooden table. The woman of the house began to come out of her seemingly abstracted state when she got a good look at the baby, and to fuss over it; after a conference with its mother, she began to prepare warm milk and bread for it in a little bowl.

The world of the dream began to blur somewhat for Dan, to blur and disappear intermittently as the woman whose body he dwelt in let her eyes close repeatedly in weariness only to have them pop open again. Dan's own mind remained impatiently alert even as the body he was in, lulled by the warmth and security of the kitchen, was drifting toward slumber in the high-backed chair.

After some timeless interval the black girl awoke with a start, at a touch from the hand of the white woman, whose kindly face was bending over her.

"And what is your name, child?"

"Oriana, m'am."

"Now you must call me Carrie. In the eyes of the Lord we are all equal as His children. Now eat a little more, and warm yourself, and there'll be a snug place where you can sleep."

Oriana turned her head, and saw that the black man had come in, and was sitting on the floor in a corner of the kitchen, warming himself with an enamelware cup of coffee, which he sipped with some uncertainty.

The dream abruptly became broken and disconnected at this point. Perhaps Oriana nodded into sleep again, and this sleep-within-sleep moved Dan's mind into some state of more normal dreaming. He saw and heard the white woman, Carrie Clareson, at the piano in the old house which then was new, a piano badly out of tune, and she was weeping as she played some noble old melody he should have recognized. And he stood beside her with a bark cup, catching blood that streamed from the arrow wounds in the side of the painted Indian girl. And . . .

. . . and abruptly the dream was clear again, and quite coherent. The three grown blacks and the infant were still waiting in the warm kitchen, but the table had been cleared, and the escaping former slaves were now all unselfconsciously sitting on the floor together while the straight chairs remained empty, and the three whites sitting around another table in the adjacent room discussed their fate in preoccupied voices. At least the two men talked, while Carrie Clareson nodded and smiled.

"It's just that we really weren't expecting three," Clareson was saying. It was a protest, though his tone was mild and conciliatory. "And now there are actually four, if the infant is reckoned in. The next conductor—well, his means of transportation are somewhat more limited than yours."

The wagon-driver, looking uneasy in a parlor, pulled at the collar of his thick sweater, and then scratched his stubby face with a work-hardened hand. "Wouldn't have a bit o' tobacco about, would ye, Brother Clareson? No, that's right, y'don't use it." He emitted a faint sigh.

"I am sorry there is none at hand to offer you. I have failed to replenish our stock of brandy, also, or I would offer you some against the cold."

"S'all right, Rev'rend. Brother, I mean. Your good woman's coffee was mighty warmin'. Now just what d'ye suggest we do? I can't very well take these folks back where they came from." The three resting, listening bodies in the kitchen stiffened momentarily.

"Certainly not!" Clareson tugged thoughtfully at his ginger beard. "Similar difficulties have arisen in the past. We shall contrive to send them on somehow. Now the next conductor—really I see no good reason not to speak his name in front of you, Brother Hollister, but it is a matter of policy—"

"S'all right, Brother, no need fer me t'know."

"—should be willing to take the *family* on entire. The infant can scarcely be reckoned as a full person in terms of food or space required. And young Oriana will be welcome to stay and sup with us until he can come back for her, or until some safe alternate means of continuing her journey should present itself."

. . . and the dream was breaking up again, spaced with bleak intervals of nothingness. Strange Indians stood in the kitchen, not breathing or moving, but yet not dead. The boy Peter ran naked and terrified across a field of summer clover . . . and then Dan was in the black girl's body in the old house once again, and the silence around Oriana was that absolute late-night stillness that only country dwellers know. Perhaps it was a different night, but anyhow the other black girl and her man and child were gone. A narrow sleeping pallet had been made for Oriana on the kitchen floor beside the stove, through whose grated door there came a glow of embers. It was a warm place, and perhaps she was more at ease with such an arrangement than she would have been in an upstairs bed.

The sound that had wakened her came again, the creak of a stair or floorboard within the house. Curled under a blanket, she opened her eyes without moving, and in a moment saw the man Clareson, dressed in his heavy coat and fur cap, pausing at the kitchen door before going out. He was looking in her direction. It was such a strange and terrible glance of pity and warning that she, accustomed to interpreting with great subtlety the expressions worn by pale faces, was upon her knees at once as soon as he had gone out and closed the door behind him. She was ready to jump up and flee, but once on her knees she paused. There was nowhere to run. Her glance darted this way and that about the room, and Dan could hear and feel the quickened beating of her heart.

There was a creaking and a thump from just outside, which Dan in a moment identified as the sounds an outside cellar door might make in being raised. This was confirmed when from beneath the kitchen there came the tramp of heavy boots descending a short stair. Then vaguer sounds, harder to make out, followed from below. Somewhere upstairs in the house a clock was ticking, an ominous sound just on the edge of audibility. The silence of the world around it seemed to hold the house bound in like drifts of snow.

Then the booted feet again, coming up the cellar stairs. And with them . . . something else.

There came in a few moments a scratching at the door, and she thought it would be a dog. There was nothing intrinsically terrible in dogs, and her fears eased somewhat. But when the door eased open and it entered, she jumped to her feet and would have run away at any cost from what she saw in the dim reddish glow that came through the grate in the stove's door. In the breathless momentary pause, the sound of soft footsteps coming downstairs from the upper floor.

The shape in the doorway, with a few stray flakes of dry, cold snow eddying after it, and now the man of the house coming in to stand behind it, was not the shape of a dog, or of any animal that had ever breathed. It was dull gray in the dim light, mottled and dirty-looking, vaguely crab-like in its numerous appendages. It was somewhat bigger than a crawling man, and now as hideously familiar to Dan Post as it was strange and terrifying to Oriana.

She leaped nimbly to get the heavy kitchen table between herself and it, and snatched up from the stove a heavy frying pan to use as weapon.

It came for her, round the table, with a dry scuttling of heavy, cloth-wrapped feet. It brought with it a vague smell of rotten grease, and the metallic-looking surface of it was shiny in spots as if with oil. The heavy frying pan slipped from her fingers as she swung it, and flew through the air to clang harmlessly from the beast's back as it might have bounced from a granite boulder. Oriana ran around the table the other way, and toward the man, who was standing inside the now-closed door with the same look of great sadness upon his face, and raising open arms that might be offering her protection. At least he was a man and not a beast out of hell. His arms closed about her and held her, while her flesh cringed to feel the rending imaginary claws that would at any moment fasten on her from the back.

But there came only a gentle touch between her shoulder blades, such as might have come from the man's finger if both his hands had not been holding her arms already. A single gentle touch and then the world tipped round her as her head fell back helplessly, her whole body going limp, its weight suddenly caught up in the hard muscles of Clareson's arms.

In the parlor, the piano began to play, an old old tune that Dan had heard before. A hymn. "Carrie," Clareson said hopelessly, almost as if to himself. "I had thought you might sleep through." And again: "Carrie . . ." in a low, despairing tone. But he received no answer, and he said no more. Holding Oriana, he managed with a little difficulty to get the kitchen door open again, and (with something heavy and cloth-footed walking after him) carried her to the outdoor cellar door, set at an angle between wall and ground. He had to set her down briefly on frozen earth while he raised the cellar door, and the icy wind tore at her bare legs and her exposed face and neck and arms. Then she was lifted again, and her limbs hung down slack and corpse-like as the man bore her down the cellar steps, now with his lantern on its wire handle swinging from his right hand. Its light danced on the cellar walls of earth, and here on one solid wall already old, a wall of stones round from the river's wear, cemented together and pierced here with a vaulted doorway, leading to a stone-vaulted tunnel, going down . . .

. CHAPTER .

5

On Tuesday morning Nancy left her apartment on Chicago's north side and drove to work as usual, maneuvering her Volkswagen on east-bound streets between Old Town and New Town until she reached the Outer Drive. Then she merged south into the eight-laned chariot race of rush hour on the Drive, whose swooping curves tore through parkland, keeping the quiescent lake in sight. Past beaches and small-craft harbors, through parks that had been defoliated of low shrubbery but not freed of the lurking violent; past statues of forgotten Germans, past deserted bridle paths, past the Skeet Club, where in an hour the shotguns would begin to pop, and fragmented clay pigeons settle in another layer upon the bottom of the lake.

She swung the small car handily through the painful S-turn where the roadway bridged the river, then worked her way over into the left-hand lane as the Drive topped a rise. The skyline of central Chicago loomed within toppling distance on her right, and the gray, classically-proportioned bulk of the Museum came into view, low and sprawling, a mile ahead.

Imperturbably sitting just where it wished to sit, taking up exactly as much room as it liked, the Museum split the superhighway into northbound and southbound vessels that went around it on opposite sides, vein and artery from the city's heart. As if it had been sitting here from ancient days, as if it waited for this culture too to ripen for the harvest, to be ingested and digested and built into the cells of specimen cases in its vast marble guts.

Nancy left the Volks in the small employees' lot and walked up the long solemn slope of steps and in, exchanging good mornings with the familiar guard at the north entrance. Inside, she walked briskly across a corner of the great skylighted central hall, whose white marble immensity dwarfed preserved elephants and even a skeletal Tyrannosaurus as well as three-story totem poles, case after case of smaller exhibits, and a scattering of early people. Then Nancy ascended by elevator to the third-floor offices.

From the large window beside her desk she had a view of the second-floor graveled roof, and across it a long row of windows on her own level. Endless cased slices of hardwood trees were visible through the nearer of those windows and gray-brown blobs that she knew were meteorites behind the farther. On Nancy's desk, besides the phone and typewriter, there waited yesterday's unfinished work. First, a small litter of letters from the public, queries from the curious on everything from fireflies to ancient Incas. There was an unknown bug in a small box sent by an Iowa farmer, and a crackpot theory, with detailed diagrams, from Minneapolis. Nancy had to see that all were answered, by the proper experts. She might reply to the Minneapolis letter herself, having acquired some competence in the field of psychoceramics. Then there was a stack of building contractors' specifications, supposed to somehow help Public Relations explain to the public the inconveniences inevitable in the next stages of the Museum's decades-long remodeling process. There were also proofs of the introductory pages of a new guidebook.

All in all it was an exciting job, a good one in Nancy's estimation, and she was glad that she was going to be able to keep it for a while at least. Of course now the needs of Dan and his family—*her* family—were going to come first. Also, if she happened to get pregnant right away, that was going to mean the end of holding a regular job, at least for as long as the baby needed her at home.

She really liked Millie and Sam, and believed off and on that they really liked her, but she thought they were probably never going to think of her as their mother. Nancy really wanted to have two more children with Dan. Of course everyone these days talked about population pressure; but Nancy had the strong but unspoken feeling that her children with Dan were likely to be superior people, very intelligent and useful to society, and that certainly ought to count for something.

Nancy was in a mood to work this morning, and attacked the pile of letters energetically. When the phone rang she looked up with a start and realized that the time for her mid-morning coffee break had rolled around already.

It was Dan's voice on the line. "Nancy?"

"Yes! Well, this is a pleasant surprise, sir. What's up?"

"Oh, I just wanted to hear your lovely voice." A few moments of humming silence passed. "I suppose it sounds kind of crazy, but I did feel a need to talk to you. Just to see if everything is still all right."

"What do you mean? If everything's all right?"

"I—don't know. I had another of those lousy dreams last night and they, they stick with me somehow. I just don't feel too good."

In the back of Nancy's mind—not really very far toward the back—a tiny but demonic suspicion was sparked into life. It was the suspicion that Dan had never been able to rid himself sufficiently of Josie, his dead wife; that for him the approaching marriage was going to be an act of infidelity, on a subconscious level at least. And as Nancy understood Dan, or thought she did, that might very well be too much for him. It could make him ill in one way or another. Hadn't he mentioned that Josie had appeared briefly, playing the piano, in one of those horrendous dreams of his?

But as yet these suspicions were not audible in Nancy's voice, nor had she even thought them out fully. She simply asked, with moderate concern: "What's wrong?"

"Well, I had another of those lousy dreams last night," It sounded as if he might not realize that he was repeating himself. "And—oh, I don't know. I don't have a fever, or pain, or upset stomach, or anything that I can really put my finger on. I suppose it's just nerves, moving into this damned house and all."

And all? Meaning marriage to one Nancy Hermanek? "Danny, I thought you liked the place."

"I did. I do. But at the same time the house is all tied up with these dreams." He tried to produce a laugh, but it didn't come out quite right.

"Oh, Dan." Sympathy and several levels of doubt were mixed up in Nancy's voice.

"I know how ridiculous it is. Look, I'm sorry I bothered you at work with it."

"Don't be silly. When something bothers you this much of course I want to know about it. I don't want you getting sick and delaying our wedding, hear? Promise me you'll see a doctor if you really don't feel well."

"Oh, it's nothing, really." And now his voice did sound much better.

"You didn't call me up just to tell me it was nothing, did you? Now honestly, Dan, I want you to have a checkup. Promise?"

"All right, promise." He sounded somehow relieved, as if he had wanted her to talk him into seeing a physician. "Maybe he can prescribe a tranquilizer or something. I'm sure there's nothing really wrong."

"Let's hope not. Who's your doctor? That fellow with some Jewish name, and his office up in Wilmette, right?"

"Shapiro. Yes, I'll give him a call. Are you coming out tonight?"

There was a pause. "Tonight's the shower, Dan. How are you feeling, really bad?"

"No!" He sounded annoyed now to the point of anger, anger with himself not her. "I just forgot about the damned shower. And I didn't mean to upset you over nothing—I shouldn't have tried to talk about this over the phone. It's nothing urgent. Go ahead and enjoy your shower, Honey. I'll call the doctor and make an appointment for a checkup, and meanwhile we're all doing just fine out here."

They went on to talk of routine things, mainly the half-dozen arrangements for the wedding that were still going to need attention. The photographer. The tuxedos. Flowers. Musicians for the reception. The invitations that had been ordered but were not ready yet. By the time the conversation ended, Nancy's suspicions had been allayed, or at least she had been distracted from them by more prosaic and concrete worries.

Nancy as usual ate lunch in the large and moderately busy cafeteria that staff shared with the public. The scientist who had made the positive identification of Mrs. Follett's projectile point saw her there and came over briefly to the table where she a couple of girl friends sat under the vast mural, more than half a century old, of a world map circa 1920.

"Got any more goodies for me, Nancy?" He was about sixty but looked younger, despite the youthful cut of his suit. On most men his age it would have had an effect the opposite of rejuvenation, but he had an inner sprightliness that carried it off. There was just a hint of some tough part of New York City still in his speech.

"Oh, hi Dr. Baer. No, but after we move in and get settled we'll certainly want you to come out and look the place over."

"I most certainly will, or else I'll send some of the young guys out. Maybe they can be more charming with your lady neighbor who owns the flowerbeds than I can." He grinned, knowing they couldn't be if they tried. "But maybe I shouldn't send 'em to the suburbs, they've all got hair like hippies." Baer himself displayed a neatly bushy set of iron-gray sideburns. He leaned on the table now, shaking his head in the negative at Nancy's invitation to sit down. "Wheatfield Park, huh? Just goes to show you what can be right under our noses sometimes. Burial mounds and Helton points. I suppose people on your block throw away a bucket of shards every time they dig a swimming pool."

Nancy said: "I don't *know* the house is on a burial mound. The rise of ground just has a certain odd look to me."

"Well, we'll sure come and check it out, once you guys grow bored with honeymooning. And stop in and tell me if you should find anything new, hey?"

Nancy was again in a working mood for the afternoon, which went by quickly for her. But because of the shower she got away a little early, fighting the small parking lot jam back onto the Drive, northbound this time, shortly before five o'clock. This time she looped off the Drive again before she had gone far, and spent long minutes creeping due west through Grant Park and the heart of the central city. Traffic gradually picked up speed as her route grew into the Eisenhower Expressway, which tunneled at ground level straight through the mountainous bulk of the main post office.

It was going to end as another warm day, though not brutally hot, and thundershowers threatened. She wished she had a sunroof on the Volks. Maybe the next car they bought would be airconditioned.

No more "the next car *I* buy." It still felt strange in anticipation, this giving over of herself to another person. Not only the body, but the name, the whole future and all its time and automobiles. It wasn't frightening, exactly, but it was strange.

Its flow loosening now to true expressway speeds, the Eisenhower bore her due west through the miles of decaying neighborhoods that stretched in that direction from the Loop. Not much to be seen, for the highway lay in a vast trench, which main north-south streets bridged at right angles. The blight was behind her before she turned off the expressway on the city's far west side, and there was no hint of its existence in the neighborhood of the restaurant where her bridal shower was being held.

While waiting for a traffic light to change, before she drove her bug across a last intersection and into the restaurant's parking lot, she lifted her eyes to the sky yet farther west. Sunset was still an hour or two away, but already the clouds in that direction were slightly reddened. Somewhere beneath those clouds lay Wheatfield Park, and in it the lives that were now of most importance to her own.

Nancy .... Dan.
She had a premonition of some kind of evil, but there was no real telepathy between her and her chosen man. Neither had words exchanged on the telephone managed to bridge the gap. She put aside as irrational her sudden impulse to forget about the shower and drive on to him at once. The light turned green for Nancy and she eased her car across the intersection, then spun the wheel to leave the busy traffic of the street. Happily she

spotted an open parking space, just beside the restaurant's door.

Dan had spent the day listlessly working around the house, or rather trying to work, though unable to accomplish very much. Shortly after talking to Nancy he had looked up Dr. Shapiro's number and called his office. He was given an appointment to see the doctor on next Monday afternoon, that being the earliest time available for non-emergencies. Six days away. The appointment made, he of course began to feel better immediately. By Friday or Saturday, he thought, he would undubtedly be in great shape. He would have to remember to call back then and cancel out.

Sam and Millie, as bona fide residents of the village, were now eligible to use the swimming pool located in its largest park, and they spent most of the afternoon there in the water—or, to hear them tell it when they came home, they spent the time standing in line waiting to get to the water.

After supper, which Dan cooked—spaghetti and clam sauce, an old family favorite—the children went out into the yard to fool around, and he did what he had been wanting to do all day, but had not yet brought himself to try. He went down into the basement to look at the old wall.

He hadn't gone down earlier because, as he told himself, to take a dream seriously enough to test it was to take it altogether too seriously. But finally Dan had to admit to himself that there was another reason for his hesitation: he was actually somewhat afraid of what he was going to see when he looked at that old wall.

To be afraid of testing a dream was even worse than testing it, and once he had put the problem to himself in those terms, he had little choice but to go down after supper.

Once at the bottom of the stairs, he stalled briefly, looking at his little plastic wine rack with its two bottles of champagne put by for house-warming. Then he proceeded deliberately across the basement to the disorderly accumulation of tools and boxes of household hardware that marked the future location of his workshop. From amid the jumble he dug out his trouble light on its long, heavily insulated cord. He had to make quite sure of what he was going to look at, and the daylight was starting to fail outside, and the only other light in the basement, a single bare bulb in an old overhead lamp, was not going to be much help.

Dan plugged the cord into an overhead receptacle and then carried its business end over to the old wall and switched it on. In the trouble light's harsh glare, the outline of the old sealed doorway was there to see on the old wall, amid its rounded stones.

Now wait a minute. He shifted the light and blinked his eyes and looked again. But there was no mistake.

At some time, evidently a time long decades past, the doorway had been filled in with stones and mortar very little different from those of the sur-rounding wall. It was in the place, and of the size, of the doorway through which he and Oriana had been carried in his dream last night. The place where the old doorway had been was not easy to see now, not even when you knew just where to look, but it was there. About five feet high and only a couple of feet wide, with its top a just-slightly lopsided arch.

It reminded Dan of one of those subtle pictures they gave you to look at in a test for color-blindness: find the doorway. Except that here the differences in color and texture of mortar between the old wall and the patch were too subtle to be picked up even by good eyes, unless you used a good light—and knew just where to look.

And he had known. Had been shown. How, and why? And by whom?

The dream promised that behind the patched-up masonry, right under the oldest part of the house where the basement did not extend, the tunnel would slant down at a sharp angle to ... to what, he didn't know. If he had ever dreamed what was at the tunnel's end, he couldn't recall it now. But presumably it was bad.

From somewhere out in the suburban streets a motorcycle bubbled and blasted, and then the evening's first ice cream truck chimed out its cheerful melody.

No. He turned off the trouble light and stepped back. Oh no. It was all utter nonsense, of course. It had had him going there for a few hours, and *really* going for a minute or two just now. But really—dreams? No. Come on. He was going to get a good grip on himself and think it all through logically.

Now, what had really happened? Obviously he had noticed this apparent doorway some time before, noticed it subconsciously or subliminally or whatever in hell the right word was, yesterday or the day before, or on his first visit weeks ago. Some part of his mind had taken note of this blocked doorway and had built it into his dreams, just as the rest of the house had been built into them. *Why* the old place should be so important

61

to his subconscious mind was a question that maybe some headshrinker would have to answer, if an answer was really required. Sure, all right, the doorway itself was real, and once it had led downward to a root cellar or something.

Dan rubbed a hand over the old mortar joints. Switching his light on again, he traced with his fingers part of the old, almost invisible outline of the lopsided arch. His nails scraped just a little sandy, bone-dry stuff from the ancient surface, and his fingers were trembling as they moved.

Good try, Danny, he thought, very logical and all that. But you're not going to be able to talk yourself out of it. Not after nightly visions like those. To call them dreams was a pretense, a mistake, though they came to him while he slept. Thinking things out was not going to make things right. He was not going to be able to get a grip on himself and proceed with his normal life until he knew the truth about that door.

He turned his head and looked at the heavy tools waiting behind the furnace, waiting as if they had been provided for this very job.

He put the trouble light down on the floor, from which angle it threw a good if somewhat spooky illumination on the work. Then, with the yard-long handle of the massive new hammer in his hands, he hesitated once again. Should he call Nancy, have her get a crew of experts in, make it a real archaeological dig? No. In the first place there was probably nothing but solid earth behind the wall, in the second place the experts would probably have a good laugh at the idea of digging in his basement, and as the clincher he couldn't wait that long. This wasn't for science, this was for his own sanity.

He fixed his eye on the middle of the blocked-up door, took a tight grip on the wooden handle, and swung the sledge home hard. The old masonry of water-rounded stones was solid, but it could not stand against this kind of assault. The first blow cracked the wall, and the second brought pieces of it tumbling down.

Once he had broken through the outer layer of mortared stones, he could see that at least the skeptical belief, or hope, in solid earth back there was wrong. Instead there had come into view a deep-looking jumble of stones and bricks, loose rubble filling a space whose dimensions could not yet be seen. When he had made a hole in the wall a little bigger than a man's head, he ceased pounding for a moment and got down on his knees to see what he could see. But even with the trouble light to help, he could make out nothing in the space behind the wall except more loose masonry, some of which had been blackened as if by fire.

Before attacking the wall again Dan paused briefly to find and put on a pair of leather-palmed work gloves. He glanced at his sport shirt and slacks and shoes and decided that they were old enough not to need worrying about. Then he set to work again with sledge and wrecking bar, rapidly enlarging the breach while being careful to keep it within the limits of the old doorway. In the old days it was a hell of a lot of work to build a wall, and usually every part of it was given something to hold up, and he didn't want to bring the house or any fragment thereof down on his head.

When the hole was big enough to let him thrust in his head and the trouble light simultaneously,

Dan froze at what he saw. He was looking up at the low, vaulted roof of the tunnel that he had beheld through Oriana's eyes the night before.

He went on working. The full shock of what he had discovered came upon him only gradually. Occasionally he would stop to stare at nothing for a few moments. Then at intervals he would set down his tools and haul debris from his excavation across the basement to get it out of the way. So far he had nothing in his rubble pile but dry stones and some blackened bricks of unknown origin. At last the hole in the wall was getting big enough to enter comfortably.

"Dad, holy gosh, what're you doing?" It was Sam, come down the stairs without his father's hearing him, so intense had been Dan's concentration.

"Sammy." Dan backed out of the hole, a couple more chunks of stone in his gloved hands. He tossed these toward his rubble pile and straightened up slowly to his full height, easing his back. Looking at his curious son, he had a sense of coming back to the sane and normal world after a terrifying visit somewhere else. But then he realized that he had not, could not, come back all the way. Something was still indefinably wrong with him. Quite wrong.

"Dad, what're you doing? You gonna dig out back there and make the basement bigger?"

"I . . . guess I just wanted to see what was back there." To Dan's own ears his voice sounded surprisingly normal. *Wasn't* he normal, after all? Wasn't this oppressive feeling of wrongness about to pass?

"Can I help?" Sam asked eagerly. He was down

on all fours now, bare-kneed in his denim shorts, peering into the opening.

"Well." Dan found he really didn't want to be alone again. "Don't get inside there. Just carry some of these chunks of rock over to the other side of the basement as I dig 'em out. Here, take these gloves I'm wearing." He half expected that the boy would tire of the job in a few minutes and go upstairs to watch television. And if it didn't work out that way, Dan decided, he would invent some other errand or task to get Sammy out of the way before the digging went much farther. Not that Dan really expected to lift up a chunk of rubble in there and uncover the crab-monster's twitching claw, no matter what the visions seemed to predict. But he was certainly uncovering the unknown, and some kind of physical danger could not be completely discounted.

Working hard, Dan dug on for a few more minutes. He could see now that the tunnel he was entering was quite short, no more than six feet or so in length, and that in confirmation of his nightmare it slanted downward sharply from the breached wall. Its farther end was against another wall or door whose nature Dan could not quite make out as yet. The little passageway was still half full of stony rubble.

In one place, he discovered, the vaulting that made up the tunnel's top had loosened enough to let a stone or two fall out of place. The electric light revealed a sheet of something greenish above the gap that had been thus created. Probing up into the hole first with fingers and then with the blade of his pocket knife, Dan found that the green was a patina on metal, on what seemed to be a sheet of hammered copper when some of the green was scratched away. As if copper sheeting had been formed into a roof above the tunnel's stone vaulting when it was made ... by whom? and when?

Dan backed out of the tunnel into his basement again, and once more stood up straight and stretched. A glance toward the basement windows showed him that it was now quite dark outside. He had put his wrist-watch into his pants pocket before starting to swing the sledge, and now he got it out for a look. Ten minutes after nine.

It was time he got rid of Sammy, but it probably wasn't going to be easy. Sam was now crouching to peer into the tunnel again. With the heavy work gloves engulfing his hands, he had labored steadily, as the growing pile of stones against the far wall testified, and his enthusiasm showed no signs of flagging yet.

"Gee, Dad, it's a regular tunnel in there. It must have been part of the Underground Railroad." Straining at prohibition, the boy moved forward until his head was inside the roughed-out doorway again.

Dan intended to walk over, take his son by the shoulders and pull him back, then send him upstairs or at least make him go and watch from the distance of the basement steps. Maybe, in fact, it was time they both quit for the night.

Dan intended so to move, willed so to move, and then discovered that his body would not obey. He could not take his eyes from the back of Sam's smudged T-shirt, could not let up the stretching effort of his own back muscles, could not adjust his own footing by the fraction of an inch. As if he were suddenly and completely paralyzed in every voluntary muscle. He had the feeling that in the next moment he might topple like an unbalanced statue, to smash in bits upon the concrete floor.

. CHAPTER .

6

Sammy continued to look into the tunnel, while from far upstairs there came the muted sounds of Millie's record player. Dan stood where he was, helpless in the grip of he knew not what. He swayed slightly, muscles adjusting to correct his overbalancing, but adjusting under some control other than his own. His back muscles relaxed and his foot slid a few inches on the floor to give him a wider and more stable stance. But he was sure that the foot had not moved at his command.

Now he willed a classical gesture of the sick and stricken, a simple raising of the hands toward the face. But his arms would not obey; they went on with a motion of their own that they had just begun, waving about uncertainly with hands at waist level, fingers groping out of control. Now he was willing to bend his knees and let his body sink down to the concrete floor in terror, but his legs in their rebellion kept him neatly balanced and upright. He wanted to close his eyes, but their lids stayed open and without his volition his gaze darted about the basement, probing at everything as if this were some totally new environment.

"Dad, what d'you s'pose is down at the other end?" Sam was halfway into the hole now, the light with him and spoke without turning around.

Dan struggled to speak, to cry out to his son a warning to get away, to run for help. But the utter helplessness of the dreams had come upon him all over again. Worse now, infinitely worse, because now it was his own body that was forced to move like a puppet at the orders of some totally alien will. He was unable even to strain his own muscles against the invisible strings.

His puppet-body turned neck and torso to complete its scanning of the basement, then walked toward the jumble of tools, bent down, and picked up what was left of a roll of twine that had done good service during the moving process. Dan's body moved a little stiffly and awkwardly, as if it were somewhat drunk, and he had not the slightest idea what it was going to do next.

Dan's fingers tested the cordage for strength, and then began to rifle his own pockets as if they were searching those of some fallen stranger. When the left hand came out with the little pocket knife, his eyes looked at it as if they had never seen it before. Then his fingers, fumbling as if they too were quite unfamiliar with the knife, got it open and cut off a couple of pieces of twine, each about four feet long.

All this while Sam was still at the excavation, studying it with the light and throwing back occasional comments over a shoulder; he was now almost completely inside the hole, and in the absence of any parental warnings to reinforce the earlier command to stay out was working his way slowly deeper.

The small pieces of twine were coiled up in Dan's left hand, and the roll was tossed aside. His eyes went searching again. What else of interest lay about? Here was a roll of black electrician's tape, whose adhesion was tested by the fingers before it went into a pocket; and here was a pair of cotton work gloves, almost new. Into another pocket went the gloves.

When Daddy's hands clamped on him from behind, Sam must have thought at first that he was only being rather roughly removed, for his own good, from the tunnel that he had earlier been forbidden to enter.

"I'm *getting* out," he muttered, half-complaining of the hard seizure, half-fearful of possibly greater punishment to come. "I'm just . . . hey, Dad! Ouch!"

Let me wake up. It was a prayer, the first real one that Dan Post had uttered for some years, and it was unavailing. He had Sammy pinned down on the open basement floor and halfway tied up with the twine before the boy fully realized that something was most terribly wrong. And by then there was no chance at all for him to make any effective struggle. His father tied him hand and foot with twine, stuffed a cotton work glove into his mouth and sealed it there with tape. His father got up then, letting him lie there on the floor making terrible choking noises, would-be sobbing noises behind his gag. Letting him lie there staring over his gag with unbelieving eyes.

Let me wake up. But even as Dan repeated the

70

prayer he knew that it was going to work no magic for him. The next thought that came to him was: then this is what happens in insanity. This is how it feels to go utterly and violently mad.

With Sam lying helpless on the floor, emitting peculiar sounds, Dan, or Dan's body, went calmly back to work to clear the tunnel. His body worked harder under his conqueror's will than it had for him, throwing rock barehanded out into the basement.

In a matter of minutes the tunnel was clear enough to provide easy access to the dark wall at its farther, lower end. The wall was somewhat convex, and when Dan's fingers reached it it felt hard, like metal or some especially tough ceramic. The faint outline of a small door was visible, occupying most of the wall inside the tunnel's termination.

Dan could see no latch or lock, but his hand under its external guidance went straight to the place on the dark metal where a doorknob might have been expected, and pressed there several times, hard and rhythmically. At once the door emitted a heavy and fearfully familiar click, and swung inward on some noiseless mechanism. Light, greenish and steady and not too bright, came out through the opening thus created. Inside, Dan saw a chamber of indeterminate size, maybe as big as a small room, half full of mechanical shapes enfolded by blank curved walls, all pale, all pastel green in the interior light.

Seemingly able to move with gradually increasing sureness under the control of the invisible puppeteer, Dan's body went back into the basement to get his son. He half carried and half dragged Sam's helpless form down through the tunnel, the floor of which was of the same gray stone that made its walls and arch. At the end of the tunnel Dan's body lifted Sam up fully into its arms and stepped into the green-lit room.

As the heavy door sighed shut behind, Dan saw that they were entering, near its top, the inside of a cylindrical room or vessel, a slightly tilted metallic silo with an inner diameter of perhaps twelve feet. The silo's bottom was at least twenty feet deeper in the earth than was the entrance from the tunnel. As his body stepped inside, Dan's feet were on a densely woven network of pale, hard rods, that like some surrealistic fire escape wound down to the bottom of the silo, leaving only a small shaft of clear space just around the central axis.

Around this stairway were curving walls, solidly lined with broad, deep shelves, which held a number of large and small containers that all appeared to be made of the same glassy, transparent substance. Dan could see very little more of his surroundings for the moment, for his eyes were now kept fixed on the footing as his body was made to begin to descend the stairs. The unwilling, twisting body of his son was draped over one shoulder. Carrying the writhing burden down the spidery, slightly tilted helix of the stairs was an awkward and somewhat dangerous task. Sam's wrists and ankles were tightly bound, but his body kept jerking, while he mumbled and groaned behind his gag.

The rod that answered for a handrail on the stairs felt strange and slightly oily in Dan's grip as his fingers slid their way along. The air in here felt so dry that it hurt his throat. Now he could see, down near the bottom of the silo, four flattened globes from which the greenish radiance came. They hung above a broad, flat table that was surrounded by other less easily nameable shapes, of furniture or machinery.

Down and around he carried Sam, around and down, amid the many crystal containers that lined most of the space along the curving walls, tier on tier of the containers like bunks in a crowded submarine or specimen cases in some strange leaning tower of a museum. Nor were the cases empty. But Dan could not turn his gaze by so much as a hairsbreadth to see what they contained.

Where the stair ended at what appeared to be the bottom of the silo, in a small solidly floored area bathed by the greenish lights, Dan's arms swung down his voicelessly protesting son and laid him on the broad table, which, as Dan now saw, was mounted on gimbals so that its surface remained quite level within this tilted place.

Sam continued trying to struggle as his father's strong arms held him on the table. Dan's eyes did not have to meet those that looked at him over the rough, taped gag, but were made to keep watching the machines that lined the curving, whitish wall along the table's other side. From amid those strange devices there now came moving out thin metal arms in several pairs. Some of the arms ended in simple metal clamps, while other carried implements more complex and exotic.

One of these, bright and thin as a needle but ending in a round swelling rather than a sharp point, fastened itself somehow on the side of Sammy's neck, and two more clung to his bare arms below the short sleeves of his T-shirt. The boy's struggles ceased almost at once; made to look down now, Dan saw his son's eyes begin to close.

Dan Post could still do nothing as his body was made to stand back and watch through open eyes. Dry air kept circulating round him gently, evaporating the sweat of work and struggle. It was somewhat cooler down here than it had been up in the house, and the air smelled neutrally fresh.

Sam had grown completely quiet now. Soon Dan's hands got out his pocketknife again, and busied themselves cutting the bonds carefully away from Sammy's limp arms and legs. Then the tape was stripped away from Sam's mouth and the gag pulled out.

The boy's breathing had by now become quite slow and faint. The clamp-handed metal arms adjusted the position of his body on the table; the sleep-inducing probes kept contact on him somewhere at all times, though individual probes at times retracted or came out again. Now, from a newly-opened panel in the wall behind the table, there emerged a thick, self-extending tube that ended in a short black nozzle. The tube moved its snout in a close oval around the short body on the table, and as it moved, continuously extruded some clear substance that looked like thickened water. After the tube's second or third circuit of Sam's quiet form, Dan realized that it was building up a wall around his son, a clear wall that might make a casket or cocoon if it got high enough.

He was not compelled to watch the proceedings any more. His body was turned around and set to climbing the tilted fire escape again, his eyes kept busy with the handholds and the stairs. His hand pulled open the heavy black door by a handle in its inner side, and he went back up through the tunnel into the basement of his suburban house, where he was made to pause and once more provide himself with handy lengths of twine and materials for another gag. Then once more his legs were made to climb.

On emerging from the basement stairs into the first floor of the house, his body stopped in the hallway and his eyes looked around, like those of a stranger entering the house for the first time. Full darkness had come some time ago, and no ground floor lights had been switched on, but soft indirect electric light shone down from somewhere upstairs, and from up there also still came the sound of Millie's record player, soft and low the way she liked it, childish voices singing incomprehensibly of love.

On tiptoe Dan's body moved to explore the ground floor, peering at least briefly into every room. Then he was made to go to the ascending stairs. On the upper floor, the three other bedrooms and the bath were briefly investigated before he was sent toward Millie's room, from whence the light and music came.

Millie was sprawled on her narrow bed in blue jeans, pink blouse, and stockinged feet, looking at a book while music played, her records and a doll or two scattered around her. She looked up casually when the figure of her father came in, but her shock when she saw his smiling face was great and instantaneous.

Millie fought him, fought hard. She was bigger than her brother, and stronger, and she was not being taken from behind and by surprise. More importantly, it was as if she knew from the first glance that a deadly enemy had come, as if she could accept at once the existence of a murderous monster behind her father's familiar face. Never mind that his face had been forced to wear an actor's smile on entering her room. She knew somehow, knew though she could not understand. Her screams rebounded from the walls and fled the house through open windows, her feet kicked at him viciously, her sharp little nails tore at his cheek. But she could struggle only a few moments before his vastly stronger arms had pinioned her, got her face turned down and pressed into the pillow and she began to smother.

With that her struggles weakened rapidly and almost stopped. She was let up for air before she quite lost consciousness, but quickly forced down again when she got out one more surprising scream and tried to renew the fight. A few moments more without air and she was helpless. Then she was gagged as Sammy had been gagged, and her wrists and ankles bound tightly with the twine.

She was still vaguely conscious, but seemingly in shock, and all the fight was gone from her as he carried her down into the greenlit hell beneath the house. There he found his son, still on the table, now almost completely sealed with a box of glassy plastic. After Millie had been set down on the table and the metal arms had come for her, one of Dan's hands reached impersonally in through one of the smaller remaining openings in Sam's glassy box, and moved one of his thin arms back and forth as if testing for muscle tone or reflexes.

The thin arm tensed slightly in Dan's grip, and feebly tried to pull away, while Sam's forehead creased in a slight frown. The boy was obviously not dead, though his chest now showed no perceptible rise and fall of breathing. His eyes were fully closed.

Dan's hands were made to remove the cords and tape from his immobilized daughter, and then his body was turned away and set to yet another task. His hands moved with easy familiarity to operate a latch that he had never seen before, and slid open the doors of a large cabinet built in against the silo's curving wall. The oily-feeling door yielded with a click and a brief hiss, as if some kind of airtight seal had been broken. Inside the cabinet, motionless as a costume hanging in a closet, the crab-machine that had pursued him through three nights of dreaming horror stood upright on its hind pair of legs.

It was a position the thing had never assumed in any of his dreams, but he recognized it never-theless. Its shape was not really crab-like, he saw now; perhaps more like that of a giant grayish-brown ant than anything else that he could think of at the moment. Its middle pair of legs, trans-versely striped like sections of flexible metal con-duit, were folded on the dorsal side of its tubular torso; and its foremost, now upper, pair of legs were bent praying-mantis fashion from where its shoulders ought to have been. No head or other sensorium was apparent from this side.

Casually Dan's hand was sent out to rub at the thing's featureless belly, which felt ceramic or metallic and seemed to be covered by a thin cak-ing of dried grime. Dan's fingers brushed at this, and then went on to feel the motionless limbs and the ball-like feet, which looked not at all like the hooves or pads Dan vividly remembered from his dreams (and yet he felt sure it *was* the same ma-chine.) From limbs and feet Dan's fingers picked up another trace or two of faintly greasy grime. Meanwhile the thing remained totally inanimate, only continuing to stand there, lifeless as a mummy or a motorcycle. Presently Dan's hands slid the doors of its cabinet closed again.

This time the fire escape was climbed unhurriedly, his body being made to pause at almost every step to look into all the glassy cases lining the walls. The lowest cases, only a step or two up from the level of the worktable and the lights, contained what looked like soil, with small plants apparently growing normally upon its surface inside the sealed boxes. Here in one box was an anthill with all its members, scattered motionless about, motionless but on their feet, like a stopped frame in a motion picture film. And here in nearby boxes were other small insects, frogs and spiders, frozen in the same eerie way.

There was a rattlesnake, coiled but appareantly asleep. With snakes it might be hard to tell, but ... other boxes held small mammals: squirrels, rabbits—and was that a prairie dog? No labels were provided. Here, inside this box, was a motionless plastic gel as clear as water or fine ice, with fish and turtles frozen in its grip, all right-side up and looking ready to go, not floating dead. And in this massive case—what? Shape like a mountain on its side, a lopsided mountain rimmed with curls of blackish hair. Was that a small up-jutting horn . . . ? Good Lord, a buffalo.

Here was a human being, quiet as all the rest, expected, but still a shock to see.

It was an Indian man, or so Dan would have described him. A man with circles and bands of white and ocher painted on his bare bony chest and wiry arms. He lay at full length, wearing only a loin cloth, supine in his transparent coffin. His chest showed no rise and fall of breathing, but otherwise he might have been merely asleep. And in the boxes after him on the ascending way, more Indians, men and women and children. Nothing but people now. The staircase was so positioned as to permit easy inspection of them all.

The first body Dan had recognized as the host of his first dream, and now another shock of recognition came, at the sight of a short casket containing a pale-skinned, naked form. The child was lying face down, but Dan recognized the bright red of the unruly hair, and the sunburned hands and neck and feet. And in the next case a boy who must be Red's companion, Peter, slept on his back, dressed in familiar homespun overalls and shirt.

There was a sudden movement up through the open middle of the silo, caught from the corner of Dan's eye, and his head was turned to watch a burden being lifted by a thicker mechanical arm than those that did the preparation down below. Sammy's casket, being hoisted into place. Dan watched his encased son go up and up, to be nudged at last onto a shelf not far below the entrance. Not a whole lot of space remained to fit additional specimens in, Dan noted. His mind was working loosely and easily for the moment, moving now in the territory beyond shock.

In the box after Peter's a blond girl lay, a teenage girl in a long dark dress, the color of youth still in her cheeks. And after her a series of blacks began. These were almost all adults, and were without exception dressed in wretched clothes. Through one man's torn shirt Dan could see how the marks of a lash crisscrossed his muscled back, wounds looking no more than a few days healed, looking still almost raw, although they must have been made more than a hundred years ago.

And here was Oriana. Though he had never seen her face before, he thought he could recognize her dress, and the shape of the body that he had temporarily inhabited.

A few more blacks, another white or two, all strangers to Dan Post, and then his son. Now he was almost at the top, the tour was over. Dan found he had been looking for two people who were not here, the Underground Railroad agent Clareson and his wife Carrie. Since Clareson was not here, might he have been the one who sealed the basement wall? Why had he done that—or why had he been forced to do it—and what had happened to him afterwards? In Dan's dream, Clareson had seemed to be working with the crab-machine and whatever master power dwelt here, in a more willing sort of cooperation than that into which Dan had now been forced . . . the chain of thought broke up, its fragments falling from Dan's mental grasp. He was still too much in shock to think coherently for long.

Standing on the entrance platform of curving rods, Dan's controlled body paused, before leaving the silo, to take a last glance back and down. Around Millie on the gimbaled table, the machines were already fabricating a new crystal box, tailored almost like a suit to her dimensions.

After closing the dark door behind him, and climbing through the short tunnel once more, Dan was made to stop in the basement. There his hand picked up the trouble light on its long cord, and his eyes studied it for half a minute. Gingerly his fingers touched the hot metal framework that shielded the bare incandescent bulb; then they found the push-button switch and clicked it off, then set the light down on the floor again.

Up on the ground floor, his body walked again through all the rooms. This was a somewhat more leisurely tour than the first reconnaissance had been. Now some time was spent in looking at the furniture, testing the locks and latches on some of the doors, and trying a light switch here and there. All the light switches were turned off again. In the living room the television set received a few moments' study—though there was no attempt to make it work—and the calendar on the kitchen wall got a steady stare.

The electric stove, the built-in extra oven in the wall, and the refrigerator were all of interest. Dan's hands worked the faucets in the kitchen sink and bathroom fixtures, on and off. The toilet also drew close attention, but was not tried.

When it had again climbed to the second floor, his body once more visited all the rooms there in turn. All were dark except Millie's; in hers a lamp still shone. Her record player had finished its program and switched itself to silence.

Dan's fingers turned the one lamp off, and then his body looked out of each of the second floor windows, one after another. From the east windows it looked long at the staccato flow of passing headlights down on Main, and at the floodlights of the shopping center on the other side of that busy highway. From a north window his eyes followed with great interest the lights of a large jet climbing away from a recent takeoff at O'Hare Field, some twenty miles away.

His hands turned on the bathroom light; then, in his own bedroom, half-lit by the reflected glow from down the hall, Dan was given a good deliberate look at his own figure in the big mirror atop the dresser. His clothes were grimy from his work, and from the struggles with his children; his hands were sore from breaking up and carrying stone, especially those last frantic minutes of labor without gloves. Sweat had mixed with dust and dirt to mat his hair and form an outer mask over an inner one, the inner one being terrible because it was formed of the very muscles of his own face, muscles that had been taken away from him and set in subtly alien patterns.

His body looked in dresser drawers until it found clean underwear. In the upstairs bath his hands had only the slightest hesitation in working drain control and faucets, getting the tub filled with water at a comfortable heat. The toilet was tested by working the handle once and observing the resultant watery turmoil; after which it was neatly used.

His body stripped and immersed itself in the tub. It soaked briefly, used soap and washcloth somewhat clumsily but to good effect, then climbed out to dry itself on a bathtowel and put on the clean underwear.

Then it walked back to Dan's bedroom and tumbled itself onto the big bed and made his limbs relax. Dan's eyes were closed for him, and he was held there in a silence that lasted for eternity before approaching sleep.

. CHAPTER .

7

On Tuesday night, Dan's fourth night in the old house, he was swept back into the Indian vision, which ran its course exactly as before, and then continued beyond the point at which its first-run showing had degenerated into a more or less ordinary and confused dream. This time while in the shaman's body he saw the crab-machine (he still thought of it that way, it was too big for his imagination to accept it as an ant) descend from the flame-walled tower through its doorway, which he saw now was the same size and shape as the dark doorway at the end of the vaulted tunnel in his basement. And still in the shaman's body, Dan knelt before the crab and anointed it with the foul contents of his bark cup . . .

. . . then befeathered warriors finished binding the stripped and painted maiden to the frame of logs, and his sinewy brown arm signalled, and the arrows flew. The crab looked on, disdainfully perhaps; not what it wanted, really, though it would let the people serve it sacrifice of this kind if they wished. But this time as the girl became an ugly corpse Dan felt only curiosity rather than terror. Reality worse than nightmares had left him numb. . . .

. . . Dan came up from an unconsciousness that scarcely felt like sleep as he pulled free of its last grip to find himself in physical control of his own movements once again. He was lying on his belly with his head turned sideways on the pillow, and there on the sheet nearby were the fingers of his outstretched hand in view. He flexed the fingers and they worked. Stupidly he brushed with them at a spot of sunlight that angled below an un-drawn shade to lie upon the bed. He just lay there keeping his eyes fixed on this phenomenon.

He had not forgotten a single detail of what had happened to him the night before. Neither could he believe for a moment that it had all really taken place.

But terrible things of some kind had happened. He felt sure of that, would have felt sure of it even if there were not such a deafening silence rever-berating from the children's bedrooms down the hall.

Dully and hopelessly he rolled over in the bed, and slowly got to his feet in his clean underwear. It was his own face, however shocked and dazed, his own face and not an alien mask, that looked back at him from the dresser mirror.

Shuffling in a daze, he went to the bathroom to relieve the painful bladder pressure that had awakened him. The light was still burning in the bathroom and he flipped it off. His mouth was very dry and there was no glass or cup in sight and he drank from the cold water faucet at the basin, and splashed some on his face. Then he walked down the silent hall and stood for some unjudgeable period of time looking at each of the children's beds, Sam's still made neatly from yesterday and unused during the night, Millie's still made but rumpled. In each room the litter of their toys and clothes and junk confronted him silently.

His own grimy clothes of yesterday were on the bathroom floor, and mechanically he picked them up and threw them in the hamper. Back in his own bedroom he found and put on a pair of clean pants, and clean socks and a different pair of shoes. Into his pants pockets he put keys and change and billfold, with some vague idea of getting himself ready to deal with the world, to face its reckoning for his crimes.

. . . his crimes. He knew that he was going to have to go down and look in the basement, but he couldn't face it just yet. If he even allowed himself to think about it just yet he would collapse. And collapsing now was the one thing he must not do— just *why* such a comfortable slide into irresponsible madness was not now allowable was another point about which thinking would have to be postponed.

Still moving like a sleepwalker, he walked down to the first floor. All around him the house was silent, warm and bright with the sun coming in under the unlowered shades. He proceeded steadily until he reached the basement door, which was standing just slightly ajar. He stood there for some time with his hand on the doorknob, unable to move the door or let it go. For the time being he was perfectly convinced of what he would see when he went down. No fantasy of ceramic silo or of crystal coffins bathed in a greenish light. No dream-stuff or crab-like machines, and blunt needles that did not pierce the body but still brought it to miraculous sleep. None of that. He knew with stark certainty that he was going to see the bodies of his murdered family where he had flung them in his raging madness of the night before. Or maybe he had broken up the basement floor or wall and crudely buried them. When he went down he might see only the mound of rubble under which their corpses lay.

At last he jerked the door wide and went quickly down the steps to see what he had done. There was the old wall, the shattered opening he had made to the vaulted tunnel, the piled debris, the trouble light still plugged in and with its caged bulb lying on the floor. His knees were beginning to quiver as he picked up the light and switched it on and took it with him into the dark tunnel with the dark door at its farther end.

His fingers punched hard at the door in the remembered pattern, and it clicked and swung back and the green light washed out from inside. Dan's knees would hardly hold him now, and it took him a moment to identify the causative emotion as relief. What he remembered was all true. It was a nightmare, but he had not killed them. In fact he did not think that they were dead. And now he realized why he must not let himself collapse.

Holding the black door open, he stepped in on the fire-escape platform. In the rays of his own light, more normal for his eyes, he saw again the spiraled ranks of crystal coffins, and the incredible machinery, all of it as real and solid as the peeling vinyl wallpaper on his suburban kitchen walls above. He saw his children where they lay encased.

Ten feet behind him in the basement were his sledge and wrecking bar. He put down the light and lunged back through the low-roofed tunnel, scrambling for a moment on all fours like some attacking predator. With snarling lips drawn back from his clenched teeth, he grabbed up the massive hammer, turned—

—and suddenly control was on him once again, an iron vise. No, stronger than that. Against iron a man could at least try to fight; he could no more struggle against this alien domination than he could escape from his own flesh.

His fingers were opened for him so the hammer-handle slid away through them, and the heavy iron head clanged on the floor beside his foot. Then his controlled body stooped and descended through the slanted tunnel again, propping the dark door open slightly with a brick, so that the trouble light could be brought in on its cord. It was left on the upper platform, filling the interior of the silo with its glare, while Dan was walked down the stairs once more, to make another inspection of the collected specimens.

Nearest the top his own children still looked as if they merely slept within their tailored coffins. Dan's eyes were not allowed to linger on them in search of signs of life, but he felt sure that their positions were at least slightly different than they had been the night before.

What he saw in Oriana's face confirmed beyond all doubt the possibility of movement among the specimens; he remembered that last night she had been lying on her back, and now she was on her right side with her knees drawn up.

Not dead, not dead. Whatever else was going on, they were not dead. Some kind of hope remained.

The inspection continued downward. Today his controller took time to study the plant and animal specimens in some detail, as well as the people, through Dan's eyes. Here was an antlered deer that Dan in his shock had somehow failed to register on his previous tour. Its head was turned in toward the wall in an expanded casket, its white-flagged rump turned out toward the stair, its brown flanks as motionless as if stuffed. And some of the smaller cases held mere twigs and leaves, in containers too small to allow for growth. These collections had no soil or water with them, nor, apparently, any steady source of light to power photosynthesis. Yet the specimens looked fresh and green enough to have just come down from daylight.

At the bottom the gimbaled preparation table waited, flat and empty and ready for more work. The thought occurred to Dan: my turn? But he was walked right past the table and made to once more open the cabinet in which the crab-machine reposed.

Now his eyes could get a better look at it, in the clear white brightness of the trouble light that shone down from above. Its body was about as big as a man's torso, and shaped like a short thick cigar. Its six legs were nowhere much thicker than Dan's thumb, and each one was segmented to be flexible throughout its length; each was two or three feet long and ended in a ball-like knob that did not seem well adapted as a foot. And Dan saw now that there was a sort of head, or at least a low, mushroom-shaped dorsal protuberance, now almost hidden behind the body as the thing stood upright on its hind legs in its case.

Today, after Dan's fingers had been made to brush at the cold, inanimate body once again, and tug testingly at one of the folded limbs—like steel cable, the leg flexed only slightly under a firm pull—they brought out his pocket knife and used it to scrape hard at several places on the crab's metal shell. The knifeblade removed nothing but traces of an old dried film, which crumbled away into faintly greasy dust when it was rubbed as if thoughtfully between Dan's fingers.

Then his hands put the knife away and closed up the cabinet again, and the puppet-strings were pulled to set him walking back up the surrealistic stair.

Gradually he was regaining his powers of thought and observation, coming out of the worst of his shock. He noted now that the progress of his controlled body was still a little like that of a cautious drunk, being made slow enough to allow for small uncertainties in the clearance of his feet on the steps, and in the pressure of his hand that gripped the slightly oily-feeling rail.

His master made him shut off the trouble light and close the silo's door, then took him out into the middle of the basement, where he was made to stand for a while looking over the confusion of excavated rubble, cardboard moving cartons, tools, wine rack, and other miscellany. He was just being made to start poking into some of the boxes when the front door's chimes sounded from above.

Without hesitation his body walked to the basement stairs and up. On the ground floor his ears got a good directional fix on the chime itself when it sounded again, and Dan was made to stand in the hall for a few moments, looking steadily up at the brown plastic box high on the wall. Then Dan was steered unavailingly to the kitchen and at last into the living room, where he saw Mrs. Follett's nicely weathered face peering in through one of the small glass panels beside the front door.

Dan's body walked to the door, fumbled briefly to release a latch whose type was evidently unfamiliar to his controller, then pulled the door open and stood there with a blank expression, waiting for whatever the woman who confronted him might do.

"Hello, Mr. Post . . . is everything all right?" Mrs. Follett, dressed for gardening as usual, blinked at him uncertainly. He could see her eyes going over him, no doubt inventorying changes substantial and small, lingering momentarily upon his damaged cheek.

"I feel slightly ill," he heard his own voice saying. No, it was not quite his own, but pretty close. "In the main, everything is well." With faintly rising hope Dan noted that the words, like the tone, were just not right. Anyone who knew him at all well must have grave doubts that this was Dan Post speaking.

Even Mrs. Follett, near-stranger that she was, peered at him closely and gave no sign of being reassured. She asked: "Are the children all right?" Meanwhile she kept darting quick little glances past him into the house.

"Yes."

She gave a little nervous, half-apologetic smile at the unsatisfying monosyllable. "I only ask because I thought I heard one of them crying out last night, well, as if in pain."

"They've gone, for a time. To school."

If this was very surprising news, in mid-July, Mrs. Follett did not show it. A subtle mask of her own control had come over her face now, or so Dan thought.

"Oh, my goodness," she commented, in guarded tones. "Well, that must have been a sudden decision . . ." She studied him in silence a moment longer, then raised what she had been carrying in her right hand, something Dan had not noticed earlier. "Nancy was so interested in that other arrowhead I gave her that I thought I'd bring this one over as well. I've been really keeping my eyes open for the last few days, and this turned up . . . at least I think it's probably an arrowhead, a rather strangely shaped little stone. How is Nancy, by the way?

"Quite well, thank you." His hand went out and took the thing without his looking at it. "I'll see that she gets this."

Mrs. Follett exchanged a few more friendly words, or tried to. She was smiling uneasily when she broke off her visit and started a retreat.

"Thank you for stopping by," Dan's controller told her in farewell. After closing the front door it could still watch her through the small glass panels beside the door, and after that through the kitchen windows on the west side of the house as she moved down the edge of Benham Road and then across her own immaculate lawn to her front door.

Don't accept it, Mrs. Follett, please, don't just let it go at that. In the prison of his own body, his thoughts if nothing else were still his property.

His body was turned away from the window, but kept in the kitchen. His fingers were made to open and close the various drawers and cabinets while his eyes inventoried the contents briefly. His hands also tested the controls of the refrigerator, and the stove controls that brought blue gas flames into existence.

At the sink, his fingers turned the water on and off, on and off, playing briefly with the stream. His controller tried the spray attachment and got a small puddle on the floor. After a hesitation of some seconds it returned him to a roll of paper towels examined earlier, thoughtfully detached one sheet, and used it to mop up the spill. Water was squeezed from the wet towel into the sink and the soggy paper then smoothed out as well as possible. It was left spread out on the countertop, as if to dry it for a frugal second use at some time in the future.

A routine itch had developed near Dan's left eye, and after it had bothered him for a few seconds his arm went up to root out the irritation with a precise small scratching. The controller, then, must feel everything that he felt, as well as seeing through his eyes and speaking through his lips. But although it could rule his body so absolutely, there was no evidence as yet that it was capable of controlling his thoughts, or even listening in on them.

Who are you? He tried to project the mental question as strongly as he could. He waited for an answer, while his body went on looking into drawers and bins, but no answer came. Maybe his question had been registered and simply ignored.

Maybe, in the estimation of his enemy, his thoughts were not worth controlling. But as long as the power of thought remained to Dan, he intended to try to use it.

Where to start?

His children were not dead, and therefore he might possibly be of some help to them. He had got that far already. What next?

Dan once again considered, and then rejected permanently, the possibility that he was simply if terribly insane; that he perhaps was only imagining he had children, or that he had really murdered them and buried them in the basement. That all the rest, the puppet-control of his body, the green-lit cylindrical vault with all its crystal caskets, were insane delusions and nothing more. Even if there was no way he could prove to himself that the insanity hypothesis was wrong, it was utterly useless. As well assume that he was dreaming somewhere and unable to awake. In either case there would be nothing he could do but helplessly endure whatever came.

There seemed to be little enough that he could do in any case, with his body so ruthlessly and rigidly controlled. But control had been interrupted once, to let his body rest in bed. Therefore some future period of freedom, some chance to act, might reasonably be expected.

Assume that he was not insane. Then what in hell *was* going on? The idea of possession leaped to mind. It was a subject that Dan Post had never given much thought. Possession was something that devils were supposed to do, at least according to some movies and some books that he had seen. Dan was no believer in devils, and hadn't been, at least not since he was very young. In God? Perhaps. At times he thought that he believed in God, a God that was beyond man's understanding, and who had no particular personal interest in mankind. But the devil . . . ? Hardly.

From what he could recall of demons and devils

in fiction, anyone genuinely possessed by these malignant, disembodied powers was supposed to throw fits, gibber obscenities, cavort like a monkey, display superhuman strength, and contort his or her body in impossible ways. What had happened to him so far didn't seem to fit the devil-hypothesis at all.

More, the strange things under his house had no connection that he could see with dark religion, magic, diabolism. They were unmistakably in the realm of technology, and it was a technology of a very advanced sort. Now before his thought there seemed to loom the domain of little green men, flying saucer stories, credulous cultists, to which he had previously given even less thought than to the supernatural.

It was still a fact, however, that he was very solidly possessed. Controlled. What did he really *know* about the controller? First, that he, or it, spoke English, though the speech was somewhat stilted and curious. . . .

His body in its restless tour of the kitchen had now come to a halt before the little cork bulletin board that Nancy had fastened to the wall to mark the spot where she wanted her kitchen phone, next to which the installer had obligingly placed the instrument. Now Dan's hand reached up to take down the little pad of paper with pencil attached that had come as adjunct to the board. Paper and pencil in hand, Dan was turned around and dropped into a chair at the kitchen table.

At this point most of his puppet-strings were released with casual suddenness. Still maintaining their control, however, were the invisible strings moving his right hand and arm. Even as he enjoyed the first deep breath of partial freedom, he watched as his right hand tore off a piece of paper from the pad, dropped it on the Formica of the tabletop, and then took up the little pencil.

His hand printed, in odd-looking block capital letters that were not his: EAT. PREPARE AND CONSUME USUAL MORNING FOOD. BODY STRENGTH MUST BE MAINTAINED.

And that was that. His hand let go the pencil and was permitted to rejoin the rest of his body under his own control. Possession had left no numbness, no pain, no detectable aftereffect of any kind. He was simply his own man again. But freedom was an illusion, of course, because there lay the paper with its written orders for him.

Body strength must be maintained. For what purpose?

About six feet from where Dan sat, the back door waited. He could get up from the table, unlatch the door, and just walk out, straight to some neighbor's house, the Folletts' probably, where he could ask for help. Or he could run when he hit the outdoors, screaming in terror and outrage until the world took notice. No need for such dramatics; there was the phone ready on the wall. He could calmly ask the operator for the police.

Remembering what had happened when he had grabbed up the sledgehammer in the basement, he thought he knew just exactly how far he was going to get in trying to alarm the world. But of course the effort had to be made. He would try the door first, he decided; why educate his evil master prematurely in how to use the phone? He suspected that was something his invisible enemy did not know, if doorbells and flush toilets were novelties.

Dan got up and walked to the door that led outside and reached for the knob, but precisely at that moment his hands refused to work for him. "All right," he said aloud. "All right, dammit, I'll eat." And at once the management of his hands was given back to him.

Moving methodically under his own control, he first put the water on for instant coffee. Should he simply fix himself coffee and toast, or a bowl of cereal? No, preparing bacon and eggs would give his hands a routine, time-consuming task and so provide more free time for his mind to try to think. Besides, his stomach had evidently been isolated from the emotional strains of the last twelve hours or so, was working on a pure brute survival level, and he was hungry for his delayed breakfast.

All right, the body strength would be maintained. Because eventually he was going to get the chance to use the body against the foe; it was an idea that he intended to hold on to, stubbornly.

Back to thought, then, while his hands were occupied with routine. His controller, whoever it was or whatever its nature, used English, but oddly. How was it odd? Well—maybe in the same way that the English spoken by the people in the dream of Oriana seemed odd to his modern senses: accent and choice of words both somewhat strange. Clareson and his wife. Maybe she had been crazy, playing the piano like that, while ... And her husband perhaps had been under this same terrible compulsion when he lifted Oriana and carried her to living death. As other blacks had evidently gone before her, not to be missed from the invisible tracks that ran escaping slaves up from the deep South into Canada. As Peter and Red had gone before the blacks into crystal boxes, evidently in the days of the first white settlements; that would have been sometime in the early nineteenth century, probably before Clareson was born; someone else had served the Controller then—yes, Schwartz, a dark and distant figure standing beside a house on this hilltop. And before that, Indians had gone, long before . . .

What had Nancy said about that first arrowhead? That it was of a type thought to be five or six thousand years old. And he, Dan, had watched the makers of the arrowhead, or their contemporaries, construct the mound in which his enemy's base still lay concealed, into which the human specimens had vanished, not for hundreds of years but thousands.

His flow of ideas was stalled, temporarily at least, by the awesomeness of the problem he was facing. But he kept trying. When his food was ready he ate it mechanically and without haste, frowning at the wall or out the window, and now and then glancing at the table where lay the little white rectangle of paper with his orders printed on it. A visitor looking in the kitchen door would have seen nothing stranger than a preoccupied man consuming a somewhat delayed breakfast.

When he had finished eating he cleared the table and then began to wash the dishes, still moving methodically, trying to postpone the resumption of control that he suspected would come as these tasks of routine maintenance had been completed. He was still at the sink when the phone rang, precipitating a reimposition of control so sudden that a plate slipped from his wet fingers to bound up unbroken from the light padding of the floor's synthetic tiles.

Completely puppetized again, his body put the

dishcloth on the counter, and traced the repetitious ringing sound to the white, complex object on the kitchen wall. His body walked over to the phone, which it had earlier looked at without touching, and his hand took the receiver down. The faint squawk of voice that followed was lifted to his right ear, whereupon the mouthpiece came more or less naturally into its proper place.

"Dan?" inquired Nancy's voice.

"I am Mr. Post," the controller answered, after a short delay.

"Well, good morning, Mr. Post. It's Nancy. Is this a bad connection or something? You don't sound right."

"Good morning, Nancy. Yes, I suppose it may be a bad connection."

"It must be. And also I think your voice doesn't sound right. Have you got a cold or something?"

"I am feeling just slightly ill."

"Oh, I bet you're not taking care of yourself. Damn, damn. Do you have a fever?"

"No, I think no fever."

"How are the kids, are they getting it too?"

"They have gone to school."

"School? Oh, you mean that day camp. I'm surprised they agreed. Listen, Danny, you still don't sound good. Anyway I'm going to run out and see you tonight."

"It's not necessary, Nancy. Not tonight. I just need some rest."

A sigh came over the wire. "I'm tired too. Maybe I won't come out tonight. Don't forget you're supposed to see the doctor anyway."

"Yes, I believe tomorrow the doctor will come."

"Come? To the house?" Nancy's voice held a

new note of alarm. "Dan, aren't you able to get out?"

"Yes, yes, of course I am."

She was growing exasperated with him. "You did make an appointment with your Dr. Shapiro, didn't you?"

"Yes." And his body's eyes moved at once to something evidently seen earlier and not forgotten, though not at once properly connected with doctors. A name and a number jotted on the wall calendar in the space for next Monday's date. "For Monday."

"Danny, are you sure you don't want me to come out tonight? Is there anything I could bring you?"

"Very good of you, Nancy, but—no. I'd rather just rest today. Perhaps tomorrow."

"Sure. You call me back if you need anything."

"I will."

"Give the kids a hug and a kiss for me."

"I will."

"Bye-bye, then."

"Bye-bye?"

"Oh, Dan, you take care. I love you, you oaf." The line went dead with a click. In a moment or so his hand hung the receiver up. Then it lifted it again and his other hand began slowly to punch out the number that had been jotted on the calendar. This time the number had been remembered, no need to turn and check it with another look.

When a girl's voice answered from the doctor's office, the voice from Dan's throat said: "This is Mr. Post. I wish to cancel my appointment with the doctor on next Monday."

That call completed, he was taken back to the sink and made to finish the dishes under control.

Then he was marched into the bathroom and forced to stand studying his face in the mirror. Rather, he was made to study a face that was his and yet not his, because the expressions it wore, trying them on now like different hats, were all subtly wrong.

If Nancy saw him like this, she would know in a moment that something terrible had happened. Millie had known, from just one glance . . . so of course the controller didn't want Nancy coming to the house tonight. But how could it hope to keep all of a man's close friends and relatives away from him?

Now as he stood before the bathroom mirror his fingertips were made to brush repeatedly at his stubbly face, and to glide lightly over the scratches that marked his cheek, which still bore traces of dried blood despite his bath. Then the fingers went back to brushing the whiskers again. It wants me to shave, Dan realized. It wants me to look normal and presentable. How did it know that he was normally clean-shaven? But that was an obvious conclusion from the shortness of his stubble; wake up, Dan. So it must want a shave, he decided; but I think I'll just play dumb. I just don't think I'll make things easy for the boss.

Control was suddenly given back to him, but he simply stood there, continuing to gaze into the mirror, trying to look dumb and puzzled. Let us see, he thought, what some passive resistance can accomplish. After less than a minute of passive resistance his body was taken over again, and the controller went back to making him stroke his cheeks.

After he had been given a second chance to understand and still refused to do so, his instructor took a different tack. It moved his left arm so that the wrist came directly under the washbasin's hot water tap, and then his right hand came across and turned the water on. Only just enough to let a very thin stream flow. The stream curved among the coarse dark hairs on his immobile arm and dribbled off, embracing an area of skin no larger than a penny.

The water was at first no more than warm, but it quickly grew uncomfortably hot. Discomfort deepened into pain, but the arm could not even quiver, much less pull away. Dan tried with all his will to fight against control, but the struggle to master his own body was just as hopeless as before. His mind seemed to be floundering help- lessly, with no way of coming to grips with its enemy.

His eyes were held riveted helplessly upon the suffering arm. He was not going to be able to scream or even faint, his throat was caught in a tight grip of silence, and his traitor legs held him mercilessly erect.

Already he was willing to give in, but there was no way to speak the words or even make a gesture of submission. The water trickled on while fine steam rose. The thought that he might be com- pelled to stand like this all day and watch his flesh destroyed was unendurable.

The punishment continued as if for a predeter- mined period of time, which objectively could not have been very long. When his enemy released him, to let him snatch his arm back with a gasp, the only visible sign of his punishment was the one precise small spot of angry red. At once he moved to run cold water on the burn.

The enemy felt the same physical sensations

that he felt—when it wanted to feel them, not otherwise. Or else it was subjectively indifferent to his pain. Bad news, either way. But what had just happened tended to confirm something that was good news, and potentially far more important: *The enemy could not directly control his mind.* If it could, it would have had no need to punish him to alter his behavior.

Good news, but not, at the moment, of much help. The eyes he met now in the mirror were his own, but changed a little for the worse from what his own eyes used to be.

"All right." It was a weary, empty voice, his own but changed a little, like the eyes. "You win. I'll show you how to shave."

He let the chilling easing water run a little longer on the small burn. Then, angry with himself for caving in so easily before what was actually a minor pain (but it had not been minor when he thought he might be made to watch his flesh literally boiled away no, not then) he walked to the upstairs bath and got out his electric razor. At once control was briefly reimposed, evidently so controller could give the device a little study before letting him use it. What did it fear that he might do? Kill himself?

Of course! Stanton, the previous owner of the house. He was probably the one who left the sledgehammer and crowbar in the basement. What was it Ventris had said of him? Nervous breakdown, something like that, and then he did away with himself. And Nancy had been sorry for unknowingly bringing up the subject as a joke.

Had there perhaps been small burn marks somewhere on Stanton's body? And how, exactly had Stanton died?

Control went away, to let him use the razor for himself, and he began to shave. If Stanton had brought the new tools to the basement, had it been with some idea of his own in mind? Or had he been acting under compulsion? Had he then found a way to kill himself, and thus escape this slavery? Or had he been tried as a tool and then discarded, his mind perhaps unable to bear the strain of mad visions and demonic puppetry?

Dan found he couldn't think it all through, not yet anyway. Right now he still had about all he could do to bear up under the strains himself. He finished his shave, looked at the results in the mirror, and then began without much thought to wash away the traces of dried blood remaining from the scratches that his daughter's nails had left. Suddenly the memory of that recent struggle became too overpowering. For just a moment he failed to refuse to think about it, and that moment's failure was too much. His image in the mirror went blurred and then it vanished in his tears.

The controller gave him a couple of minutes (had Stanton been denied even that much relief, an ultimately poor economy from the controller's point of view?) and then shut off his tears as if by a turned valve, and in the middle of a ragged sob it took over his lungs and throat to form a deep, calm breath. It casually wiped his eyes and finished the little clean-up job on his scratched cheek. Then, tightening or loosening his facial muscles one by one in small increments, it little by little expunged the frozen look of suffering from his face.

The puppet face in the mirror was not that of the real Dan Post, not quite yet. But already it was getting closer.

▪ CHAPTER ▪

8

Wednesday morning's mail still lay unopened on Nancy's desk, though lunchtime was approaching. The little red book was in her hands, and she was staring at it. Her neat mind, used to sorting out problems into their proper compartments as a first step in solution, was stalled on this one. If this had come in as a question from the public, she would have had to reply that there was no Curator of Strange Old Diaries, not at this museum anyway. Try the Historical Society.

Of course her real problem was not just the book itself, but the book and Dan. But consider just the book, which was all she had in hand to study at the moment. The first question that came naturally to mind on reading it was whether or not the woman who wrote it was insane.

Consider the first entry, dated May (or perhaps March, the writing was quite poor) 10, 1857. In it the woman who kept the diary lamented over the arrival "last night" of "more passengers" who, she was sure, were likely to be "bound to the devil, some of their number if not all." And in a June entry (the woman had used the diary only sporadically, evidently as an outlet for her troubled mind) it was specified that "he" (in context, only the devil could be meant) dwelt "right under the house."

The mention of "passengers" would seem to connect the book, and therefore the house, with the Underground Railroad, in confirmation of the local folklore that the real estate agent Ventris had once mentioned. Only two names were mentioned in the book. There was passing mention in a couple of places of a man named Schmiegel (that seemed to be the spelling) and his family; Nancy got the impression that Schmiegel was some kind of a tenant farmer or renter of land from "James", the husband of the diarist.

And James was the key to it all. The woman mentioned several times the great lengths she was going to, trying to keep the diary from falling into his hands—how after every entry she crept up into the attic and hid the book behind the chimney there. The strain on her had undoubtedly been terrible, whatever its real causes may have been. The entries in the diary became progressively more incoherent, and the writing worse, until at last it was almost completely illegible.

The part that held Nancy back from going to work was decipherable, though, after she had puzzled over it for a while. It was part of the entry for October 12, 1857, which discussed at greater length than ever before James's "hideous bondage"—apparently to the devil himself, "—it began with his smelling strange odors, as our fathers might have ascribed to Brimstone from the Pit. And he was afflicted with terrible dreams, of Indians and their savage rites carried out in unknown tongues, and of a devilish beast or creature that they worshipped. I have no one to tell these things, nor would anyone any longer believe that Satan comes to take possession of a Christian soul, such as James was when first we came here and he rebuilt this house. . . ."

There was more, but that was the heart of it. Smelling strange odors, and afflicted with terrible dreams, and then hell somehow took over, and more victims were bound to the devil. Nancy shook her head, put on a self-deprecating smile to see how it might feel, and put the book down. She took up and opened the first envelope of her mail, and skimmed twice through the letter inside without being able to understand what it was about. Hopeless.

Red book in hand, she headed down the corridor to look for Dr. Baer.

As soon as Dan had finished his morning chores his master took him on another tour of the windows on the second floor, to make its first real, daylight survey of the surrounding neighborhood. A passing aircraft was even more interesting than last night's, that had been visible by its lights alone. Another sight that for some reason drew the controller's prolonged attention was that of a nursing home located about a block and a half to the northwest; there a trio of whiteheaded elders were visible through some intervening tree branches as they sat quietly on a porch.

As usual, the greatest amount of activity was to

be seen on the east side of the house, looking toward Main Street. Here Dan's eyes were kept turned for the most part on the vehicular traffic, but were diverted to examine male pedestrians whenever any of these came into view.

After a quarter of an hour or so of observing the outside world and its people, his eyes were turned downward to consider his own dress, T-shirt and wash pants. It seemed to Dan that he could almost hear the controller's following thought: *Not quite right for going out.*

It walked him to his room and got a sport shirt from a hanger in the closet, and then gave him back control of his arms. The small burn on his left wrist still sent its warning signals along his nerves. Without hesitation, he put on the shirt. It looked as if they were going out.

Maybe they were, but first it took the time to scrutinize the contents of his pockets carefully, paying particular attention to what it found in his billfold. The money—about thirty dollars—was rather cursorily examined, but the credit cards were quite intriguing, judging by the amount of time that he was made to spend looking at them and feeling their embossed surfaces. Intriguing also were his driver's license, and his insurance and social security cards. The photographs of his children were of interest too, perhaps purely technological. His controlled fingers bent the pictures lightly and rubbed them, then held them up close before his eyes as if to study the grain of the print. He carried no photograph of Nancy. So far he had only the framed eight-by-ten of her at his bedside . . . he seemed to recall that it was now lying face down on the night table, probably brushed against and knocked over when the enemy had dropped him into bed for his first night of enslaved rest, or by his outflung hand in some subsequent tossing as he slept.

When its inspection of his pockets was over, it walked him downstairs and to the front door. He felt a faint satisfaction as his prediction that they were going out was proved correct. Then, much to his surprise, just at they reached the door it let him go.

He was wary. Obviously he was being tested. He knew that control could be clamped on again with electric speed, and he believed that punishment would follow his least attempt to thwart the enemy's will. Still ... suppose, just suppose, that it would let him get into his car and drive. Let a police car come near him when he was driving, and he would ram it. Let a traffic light be red when he approached, and he would sail right through. He would get himself under the close scrutiny of the authorities; he would get himself locked up where he could do no further harm, and then he would try somehow to reveal the truth. Maybe the enemy would have effective countermeasures to employ, but Dan told himself that it was worth the risk. He had to see if it would let him drive.

Dan stepped out of the house and pulled the front door shut behind him. Ordinarily he would not have got out his key and double-locked the door, but on impulse he decided to deviate from normal behavior on this point. Dan walked on, slowly, and felt a small sense of success when his deviation apparently went undetected. His steps were not directed. It was waiting to see what he would do.

He strolled around to the garage and got his keys out and took the padlock off, and with the requisite lift-and-tug swung open the old doors. It then allowed him to open the car door, and get in on the driver's side, but that was all. Transition to total control was very smooth this time, as if the enemy's use of his body, that had at first been an unfamiliar implement, was improving rapidly with practice.

For several minutes the body of Dan Post sat in the left front seat of Dan Post's car, carefully looking over all of the controls and indicators. Dan's hands were kept immobile at his sides, and his feet were not allowed to get too near the pedals on the floor. Then his body got out of the car and carefully closed it up again, using the key to lock the door rather than the simpler but unlearned expedient of pushing down the button before it was slammed shut. The garage doors were closed up neatly, and the padlock fastened on them as before. By this time Dan was afraid; what now, back to the hot water tap?

But evidently his master did not mind that he had wanted to drive the car. Maybe it appreciated being shown something so interesting. Anyway he was not being taken back indoors but out for a stroll, on the grass border of Benham Road. After a moment's hesitation there, looking to left and right, his body was steered left, toward Main.

Nice sunny day. Dan's neighbor on the east, he of the four-bedroom ranch, whose name Dan could not manage to recall, was out doing something in his yard. Dan's face smiled a controlled greeting, and his right hand went up in an awkward-feeling, uncharacteristic wave. The neighbor returned the wave uncertainly and with the briefest answering smile.

Dan's body continued walking along the grassy

border of the road, heading east toward Main a block away. For whatever reason, the power in charge suddenly gave him back control of his upper body while it kept his legs strolling along in the direction it had chosen. Getting fancy now, like some skilled musician grown accustomed to an instrument.

When he had reached the corner of Main and Benham it turned him southward for a block, walking the sidewalk slowly between the suburban lawns on his right and the four lanes of traffic on his left. It kept his eyes busy observing the traffic, with time out to read the road signs and also to scan the activity of the cars and people moving about the shopping center on the other side of the highway. After about a block of this it walked Dan over to the curb and reassumed complete control. When a lull in traffic came it marched his body briskly across the busy road.

The small elation he had felt on being able to leave his door unlocked was by now buried out of sight in deepening gloom. The thing seemed to be learning with disheartening speed. Whatever ignorance of the modern world had hampered it at the start, when it first seized him, was fast being replaced by knowledge.

It continued to show an interest in aircraft—here came another one now, and he was made to stop on the east side of the street and gaze at it. And it was unsure of itself with regard to electric lights and electric razors and automobiles. And telephones, though that had been quickly learned. On the other hand, it spoke English, though its choice of words and its accent were rather odd.

Nothing physical had come charging out at him when he broke down the basement wall. But something had come out, all the same. Some intelligence. Some power, that perhaps had slept there for a hundred years or so, cut off from the world. Why had it come out now? A random choice, or—what?

Before Dan Post, it had tried to use Stanton to break down the wall for it. And what Stanton had experienced had made him choose death instead. Or for some reason he had been found wanting, and had simply been thrown away . . .

It walked him about the shopping center, avoiding moving autos skillfully and looking into the various store fronts. It did not stop long to gawk at anything, and it was hard for Dan to tell just which of the stores it found most interesting. It hesitated briefly in front of the supermarket, and then it marched him in and they began to shop.

To Dan it seemed that his body's behavior in the food store was somewhat peculiar, and the faint hope began to rise in him that he and the master were going to draw suspicious attention. It made him peer a little too carefully at everything and everyone. It made him stand quietly studying the cash register from a little distance, until it seemed to him that the checkout girl might well take him for a potential bandit, and notify the manager, but her brown eyes were far away, on some deep dream or problem of her own. And the enemy at first ignored the shopping carts, then made him retrace his steps to get and use one. But soon Dan realized that he was wrong to pin any hopes on these small peculiarities which no one else seemed to notice. The world was full of people behaving far more oddly than he was, and being suffered to go their ways unmolested and unnoticed.

Sure enough, his slight awkwardness in parcelling out money for his modest bag of groceries drew no one's attention at all. He realized as the girl was bagging his purchases that he had bought nothing but duplicates of containers that were already in his kitchen cabinets or refrigerator, and on their way to being depleted.

Outside the store, his body paused to watch and then imitate a man buying a newspaper from a vending machine. Then his feet were steered casually but safely back across Main. Not right back to the house, though. When his feet reached the corner of Main and Benham, they kept right on walking north. It seemed that there was going to be a little tour of the neighborhood.

The chief goal of the tour proved to be a close inspection of the nursing home that he had been made to stare at earlier from his upstairs windows. Now his body almost loitered on the sidewalk right in front of the place. He strolled with a slow pace that was almost a mockery of the inmates' shuffling, and eyed with an almost hungry gaze a nonagenarian curled in a chair on the old wooden porch.

God, why couldn't it have made him dawdle suspiciously before a playground or a school? Then the police might soon be on their way to check him out, or at least some curious neighbors would have taken notice and might be watching to see what he did next. Now his eyes were probing eagerly at a man standing on the porch, man ancient and withered, who supported himself with a knobbed cane and chewed his toothless gums.

Why was the specimen collector browsing here? Well, among the occupants of the crystal cases (he had them all plainly in front of his mind's eye, and would until the day he died) there were fair samplings of most human age groups as well as several races. But, for whatever reason, a representative of senility was missing. Maybe the senile humans did not keep well, would not stay fresh more than a century or so, in that peculiar root cell underneath his house . . .

When one of Dan's arms began to tire, holding the bag of groceries, the controller obligingly shifted it to the other. No gratuitous torture for the good slave. Dan was marched once around the block that the nursing home (which fifty years ago had been someone's impressive residence) stood on, and then hiked back to his own house. The little game of leaving the front door only half-locked had been fruitless; there were no burglars inside to complicate the controller's problems.

Once inside, Dan was released for a program of personal maintenance and lunch. At least he began to occupy himself with these matters, and was not overruled. Good. Time spent on familiar physical routine was probably the only time in which he was going to be able to think.

. . . what lasts for a thousand years or more, sealed up in a vault, and has an excellent memory? Some kind of an advanced computer, was the only answer that came to mind.

If it had been built a thousand years ago or more, it hadn't been built on Earth. The silo was a spaceship, or part of one at least. It was what Earthmen, when they were on the other end of the operation, called an unmanned probe, a machine programmed to gather knowledge and specimens from some alien planet. Except that whoever or whatever had sent this one evidently thought in terms of millennia rather than mere years or decades as the proper length for this sort of mission.

Perhaps the probe beneath his house was sending data home by radio. Or, perhaps more likely, by some other means as unimaginable to twentieth-century man as radio would be to men of the Stone Age. But it was gathering and preserving specimens physically, too, which strongly implied that someday, at some pre-programmed time perhaps, or when its storage space was full, it was going to take them home with it. Wherever home might be—maybe thousands of years away among the stars. Dan shivered in the July day.

Great care was obviously being taken with the specimens. They were not simply being kept from decay. Their bodies moved, as if they only slept inside their boxes. In some sense, he was certain, Sam and Millie and the others were still alive. But, looking at it coldly, were they, could they be, restorable to full human function?

He didn't know. He couldn't guess. The level of science that held life so suspended for hundreds and thousands of years was so far beyond the levels of the twentieth century that it might as well be magic after all.

With such powers arrayed against him, what chance was there that he would ever get his children back? He only knew that he must make every effort, give his own life up if it would help.

When he had finished cleaning up after a very informal lunch—cheese sandwich and pickles, and a glass of milk—it took him over again and sat him down in the living room to study the newspaper it had purchased. As he read under control, he soon found that his eyes were skipping across the columns and up and down the page faster than his own mind could keep up, ahead of the ability of his brain to make sense of what they saw. With a sinking feeling Dan understood that the enemy could read English considerably faster than he could. And he was not, by ordinary human standards, a slow reader.

Interrupting this speed were fairly frequent delays of two or three seconds each, caused by words belonging to modern science or technology. Phrases such as "nuclear power station" or "solid state" or "energy crunch." And it was science and technology that got the enemy's closest attention, by far, though every article, cartoon, and advertisement in the paper received at least a glance.

Politics got the merest skimming; Dan's controller cared not much for the humanities, nor for news of the endemic warfare that Earth still wore round her equator like an eruptive rash. The photograph of a tank, part of an armored column ravaging some Middle Eastern land, received close scrutiny, though. So did the faces of the victims of a Japanese earthquake, however, and there was nothing of science or technology apparent there.

His controller never bothered to look at a clock or watch (Dan's own wristwatch had been lying on his dresser in his bedroom since last night) so it was hard for Dan to judge the passage of time while he was under control. But sometime toward the middle of the afternoon the newspaper reading was completed, down to a scanning of yesterday's race results. Then Dan's hands were made to thumb back through the pages to the television log.

Obviously the controller had managed to make the connections between the program listings in the paper and the squarish, glass-fronted box that stood in a corner of the living room. After a minute or two spent in examination of its controls it got the thing turned on and tuned in and sat Dan down in front of it, close enough to reach out handily for frequent channel-switching.

A baseball game from Chicago was soon rejected. A soap opera was considerably more interesting; the controller was content to listen and listen as the characters talked and talked. Nor did the controller's attention flag during commercials.

After one soap opera came another, until eventually the children's programs began. Brats of the 1930's cavorted improbably in old films and then their modern descendants, mixed in with furry puppet-monsters, appeared to do their thing on videotape.

When a man's face appeared to say that it was time for the six o'clock news, Dan's master made him reach out an arm and snap off the set. Control went off at the same instant, so suddenly that his extended arm fell thwack against his chair. Evidently it was time again to maintain the body's strength.

He had just gotten to his feet, wondering prosaically what he should have for dinner, when the front doorbell rang, once and then twice more in rapid succession, and control was back on him with the swiftness of a sprung trap. Under total control his body moved to answer the door.

At six o'clock it was still bright summer day outside. On the porch waited two solid-looking men with business-like eyes. They wore sportcoats over open-collared shirts; the younger of the two was very large.

The older one flashed something in his hand at Dan. "Mr. Post? We're from the police. Mind if we come in?"

Dan's body had frozen into immobility in the doorway. "What's it all about?" his controlled voice asked. The voice spoke more rapidly now, Dan noticed, and with a more modern accent. Meanwhile Dan's mind felt faint, was holding its psychic breath against the impact of what looked like imminent salvation.

"We just have a few questions we'd like to ask. It's concerning your children."

There was a pause, a pause that Dan felt was too long by normal contemporary human standards, but might have been just right in one of the afternoon's soap operas, wherein non-events were stretched and padded out to fill a measured chunk of real time. It would have to give the game away now, by one blunder or another. Dan had the feeling that his relief would have made him weak in the knees had not his knees like the rest of his body been seemingly disconnected from his mind. *Mrs. Follett, you did come through. God bless all nosy neighbors, forever and ever amen.*

"What's happened?" Dan's lips asked, at last.

"Can we come in?"

Stiffly his body made way for the two detectives, while his eyes gauged them, their size and bearing, the way they walked. Then, looking out, he saw their unmarked car in front of the house, parked in a slightly careless fashion with a rear fender sticking out onto the pavement. Dan's eyes rested momentarily on the microphone of the car's two-way radio, which was just visible, along with a small curl of insulated wire, above the dash.

If the controller had any personal emotions, they were being kept under control just as firmly as were Dan's. Dan's hand closing the door behind the police was perfectly steady, as was his voice when he turned to confront them inside his house.

"What's happened to my kids?"

"Why do you think something might have happened to them, Mr. Post? Lots of times we call on parents just because their kids have gotten into trouble of some kind."

"My kids don't perpetrate any crimes. Now what's wrong?" The voice was still wrong, for one thing, and the choice of words still not really right. But good enough, maybe, to get by.

The older man, who was doing all the talking so far, softened his own voice a bit. "We're just trying to find out if something might have happened to them, Mr. Post. Now you have a girl and a boy, don't you? Millie and Sam?"

"That's right. What's happened?"

"And where are Sam and Millie right now, Mr. Post?"

"At this moment?" *God bless you, Mrs. Follett.* He was saying it over and over in his mind. "I had thought they were in school. Do you tell me now that they are somewhere else?"

"Mind telling me just what school they're attending, Mr. Post?" These two men looking at him so steadily from behind the casual questions were not going to be put off with casual lies, and they were not going to be overpowered and dragged into the basement, either, not by one Dan Post-model puppet. Were the crab's feet moving now upon the basement floor, softly coming toward the stairs? Odd, ball-shaped feet that didn't fit . . . his body was talking again:

"Sit down, gentlemen, won't you? I'll try to answer all your questions. But it may take a little time." Dan's body calmly took a chair for itself, even as his hand gestured stiffly toward seats for the others. Even if the crab should climb the stair and strike, there was the car outside. If these men did not get back to the station on schedule, or call in, others would soon be coming to find out why.

"Thanks, we'll stand." The older, graying detective continued to do the talking, while the huge young one hovered in the background, hands behind his back or loose and ready at his sides. Both of them were looking at Dan with open suspicion now, while he sat regarding them with what felt like an open, friendly look but gave no information.

"Mr. Post, can't you tell me what the name of your children's school is? And when you saw them last?"

"Of course. I saw them no more than a few hours ago."

"Some time last night?"

"Why, no. This morning."

"Before they left for school?"

"Officers, if you'll tell me just what this is all about, perhaps I can be more helpful."

"You were going to tell me the name of their school." The graying detective changed his mind about sitting down, and sank into the chair opposite Dan, running a hand wearily over his forehead. Maybe it had been a hard day, fighting crime in the peaceful suburbs.

"Did you hurt your face somehow?" put in the oversized partner, unexpectedly, from his looming stance in the background. "You have some scratches there." Now the big man too was rubbing at his own eyes.

"Yes," said the voice from Dan's lips, and with that a brief silence fell.

119

The older man's eyes were boring steadily into his, waiting to be told the name of the non-existent school. It's all up with you now, controller. Throw your weapons down. . . . In the prison of his own skull, Dan was thinking bleakly that the thing probably had available some way of killing him rather than let him go; and it might kill its specimens, too. But its secrecy was destroyed, its mission ended. Now it faced no primitive, struggling village or isolated farm. In late twentieth-century America it faced too many brains and weapons, too much organization. . . .

The older detective was speaking again, but in the fullness of his relief Dan was not paying attention enough to understand the words. Then abruptly Dan realized that control had been lifted from him. He jumped to his feet.

The older policeman did not react to the movement. He only continued to sit in his chair, still gazing intently at the chair where Dan had been. He was nodding gently now, a mild smile on his lined face. The big young cop was leaning now against the mantel, and also staring steadily at nothing.

"Listen!" Dan grabbed the big one by his sport-coat sleeves. Like trying to move an offensive tackle out of his place. "Snap out of it! Help me! My kids are being murdered in the basement!" The big guy almost toppled from Dan's pulling and shaking, then stuck out a powerful arm and pushed Dan's hands away, meanwhile continuing to gaze off into the distance, where something most entrancing was.

Dan spun away and grabbed at the older man, lifted him right up out of his chair with a grip on shirt and arm, shook him limply like some rag-stuffed tackling dummy. But the detective was not provoked into response. When Dan let go he slid to the floor in a collapse with his head down, rump elevated, like a sleeping baby.

Almost sobbing now in incoherent rage, Dan turned from one of the detectives to the other, kicking and cursing and slapping at them, to no avail. Then he suddenly thrust a hand inside the bigger detective's jacket, reaching for the holster that he assumed was there. He had guessed right, but his fingers had no more than touched the hardness of a gun-butt before total control was back again, clamping his hands and arms into a statue-like rigidity. Thrown off balance, he toppled to fall beside the other man on the floor. A scream of despair was choked in Dan's throat before it could begin.

Then, moving smoothly under total control, Dan's body got to its feet and looked around. It walked to the windows and looked out. The police car still waited beside the street. The world outside was undisturbed and unalarmed.

At a rustling of clothing behind him, his body turned. The police were both standing up straight again, casually adjusting rumpled clothes and brushing themselves off. Their eyes were in focus once again on Dan's, but their faces were still in strange repose.

"Sorry to have bothered you, sir," the older one said. He gave Dan the abstracted smile of a busy man whose mind has already shifted to some future task. He and his partner began to make their way toward the door.

"Wait, officers." Control was still willing to let Dan talk, although he could not move. "My children. Save my children." His voice was unrecognizable now, less like his own than was the enemy's impersonation. "Save them, they're still alive, I know it. Down under the house."

"That's quite all right, sir. No trouble at all."

"Under the house, under . . ."

"Thanks for your co-operation." Nodding and smiling, they went out, pulling the front door carefully shut behind them.

Before their car pulled away, his body walked to a window from which it could observe the Folletts' house. There was the telltale twitch of curtain.

.CHAPTER.

9

When it let go of Dan again he went straight to the kitchen cabinet in which he kept his small supply of booze. If memory served him right, there should be a fifth of bourbon on the shelf, still about half full.

His memory was correct. But no sooner had his arm brought the bottle out than it was stopped by the puppet-strings. The bottle was moved up carefully before his face, and his eyes were made to scrutinize the label thoroughly.

"I tell you you'd better let me have this," he muttered savagely to his unseen master. "Better let me have it, if you want me to keep functioning at all."

After it had studied the label, and used his nose to sniff the contents, it turned him loose. At once he reached for a shot glass and poured himself a drink and downed it, neat. Ordinarily he never could have taken whisky that way, but right now it tasted like so much tea.

Fighting back an urge for the cigarettes that he had given up five years earlier, Dan brought the bottle and glass along and went to sit at the kitchen table. On the table still lay the pencil and pad of paper that had been used in the morning's seance.

"All right," he said quietly, looking down at his hands folded before him. "So you want me to keep functioning, for a while at least. That means you want me to help you in some way." He took up the bottle and slowly poured himself another shot. No, only half a shot this time. "Somewhere along the line, in whatever you're planning next, you're going to want my willing co-operation. Or at least things will be easier for you if I can be brought to co-operate. Right?"

No answer. He looked at his hand and at the waiting paper, but nothing happened.

Dan took a sip from his glass, and sloshed the liquor around inside his cheeks like mouthwash. "There is something I need, too. Maybe we can trade." He paused. "I want my children back, alive and—essentially unharmed. For that I'll be willing to cooperate. I'll help you get other people to replace them, if that's what you want."

He drank again. He wondered now, with sudden understanding, how often the enemy might have heard this same speech. From Clareson, from Schwartz, the one the farm boys said was crazy. No doubt there had been others.

His right thumb gave a little preliminary twitch, and then his hand took the pencil up. It lettered, OFFER TENTATIVELY ACCEPTED. WE WILL NEGOTIATE.

His reply was quick: "First, how do I know you

can deliver? How do I know they're not already dead down there?"

IF THEIR VIABILITY CAN BE DEMONSTRATED, ARE YOU THEN WILLING TO HELP ME COLLECT MORE SPECIMENS?

"Yes. Yes." He would promise it anything, and at the same time allow himself no shred of comforting belief in anything it promised him. Clareson and Schwartz and their families, how did they wind up?

Dan suddenly recalled the diary, the first time he had thought of it since he had fallen into the controller's grasp. It was dated in the 1850s, which must be about Clareson's time. Dan had only scanned it very briefly, before giving it to Nancy, and now he could remember practically nothing of its contents. Anyway Nancy had it now, and it just *might* be of some help . . .

GET THE NEWSPAPER. It always neatly penciled in the proper punctuation marks. Dan wondered why it preferred to put its communications down on paper rather than make him talk to himself. Maybe it had tried the latter method on some of its victims only to find it brought their mental collapse on sooner and more certainly.

When he came back to the kitchen table with the newspaper it took over his hands with seemingly impatient speed and turned the pages rapidly. It remembered exactly the pages it was looking for.

First it turned to the Japanese earthquake pictures on the back page. With the pencil it drew an almost mathematically precise circle around each of the Oriental faces that were plainly visible in the photos. Then it lettered in the upper margin of the page: SPECIMENS OF THIS RACIAL GROUP ARE HIGHLY DESIRABLE.

The face of the Japanese woman turned toward the camera, contorted with her pain and grief, was suddenly Nancy's face. What if she took it into her head to come out tonight after all? Or tomorrow she would certainly come, unless he could phone her, invent some story, provoke a quarrel, anything to keep her off. Could he make up some convincing explanation for his master, that would let him call her tomorrow morning and get her to stay away? . . . but right now negotiations were in progress, he had to follow what it was doing with the paper. Again his hands were rapidly turning pages, this time stopping at an article about the plight of the aged in their nursing homes. Again there were photographs.

ALSO ONE OF THIS DEGENERATED BUT PRESERVED CONDITION. EITHER SEX. ANY RACIAL GROUP.

His hands were released. It was his move now.

He picked up the whisky bottle, looked at it, then recapped it firmly and took it back to the cabinet. Then he turned to face the empty room and asked: "And if I help you get these—specimens—you want, will my children and I be left completely free? What I mean is, are we supposed to go on living here with—that—beneath our house?"

He got no answer until he remembered to walk back to the table where the pencil and paper were.

IF YOU HELP ME YOU AND YOUR CHILDREN WILL BE SET COMPLETELY FREE IN A MATTER OF DAYS. THE TIME IS NEAR FOR THIS COLLECTOR OF SPECIMENS TO DEPART.

From behind him Dan heard the basement door click open.

He turned in his chair, and was then held motionless, this time not by any external influence. Sammy stood in the kitchen doorway, palefaced and slumping against the wall. His white T-shirt bore the marks of the struggle on the basement floor, but his arms and neck showed no marks where the blunt needles had adhered. The boy was alive and himself, but himself as he might have appeared after a long illness. Illness was suggested not by any real wasting of his body, but by his slumping pose and by the pallor and the expression of his face.

"Daddy?" the voice seemed to come from the babyhood of years ago. "What's wrong? I had a terrible dream . . ."

Dan moved now. But even as he lifted his son up in his arms, he felt the control of his arms being taken effortlessly away from him. They now supported Sam's weight impersonally, and Dan's controlled legs now walked back toward the basement door.

"Daddy, I feel all pins and needles . . . I had to climb out of that box . . . Daddy, no, don't put me back in there again . . ." But this time Sam was too weak to put up much of a fight. He could only cry, weakly and uselessly, as Daddy's arms bore him back down the basement stairs and then once more down into the alien place beneath.

Sam's crystal box was waiting on the gimbaled table, under the green lights, its top swung back as if on hinges although there were no hinges to be seen. Dan's body put him in and then stood back at attention while the blunt-needled probes came out once more from the wall. This time the process was swifter than before. In less than a minute the box had resealed itself, leaving no visible seam, and Sam was being swung away in his terrible sleep to hang with the other specimens against the curving bulkhead of the alien ship.

This time Dan was not released on parole until he was halfway up the basement stairs; he continued the climb himself, with scarcely a break in stride.

In the kitchen he stood at the table, looking down at the newspaper with its circled faces, and at the printed orders that the enemy had so confidently omitted to destroy. But it was not omnipotent, or it would not want his help.

At last he said: "All right, I'll accept that you can restore my children to me. So I'll help you. What must I do?"

SUGGEST A PLAN FOR OBTAINING THE SPECIMENS I WANT.

He sighed. He hadn't expected this. "You're going to have to let me think about it a little," he said at last. "It won't be easy to just—obtain people. It isn't possible to simply buy them anymore, you understand. At least not in this part of the world."

He sat down at the table and picked up the pencil and toyed with it in his fingers. Outside, the sun was lowering into the treetops just behind the Folletts' house.

He said: "If you want me to devise a plan, I'll need more information on what kind of powers I'm working with. Your powers, I mean." A pause, with nothing happening. "I know you can control people's bodies as you do mine, and also people's minds, as you did the police. But there must be some limit, or you wouldn't want my help. For example, I don't suppose you can force some nurse over there at the nursing home to just wheel some patient over here for me to put into the vault; and then force everyone to forget that that patient ever existed."

While he was waiting for an answer he was thinking also that the enemy might very well have been telling him the truth about the time for its departure growing near. As he had seen, its specimen racks were now nearly full. Also—and this was just a hunch on his part—it might want to go because it had now observed a really radical change, a quantum jump, in the nature of the organization of human life upon this planet. In the few decades since the 1850s the people of the planet had bound themselves together in networks of communications and transport much tighter than any known before; they had sent their representatives into outer space; and they had begun to gain great powers not only over the gross physical world, but over the world of knowledge, of information-handling, in itself. Such radical changes might well be of more than passing interest to whoever had designed the probe and sent it here.

This time Dan was kept waiting for his answer for nearly a full minute. It was a much longer pause for thought than any that the enemy had taken before. But at last Dan's right hand was made to reach out for the pencil.

THERE ARE INDEED LIMITS TO MY ABILITY TO CONTROL. ONCE PHYSICAL CONTROL HAS BEEN ESTABLISHED, AS IN YOUR CASE, IT CAN BE MAINTAINED AT VERY GREAT DISTANCES. BUT TO ESTABLISH PHYSICAL CONTROL OVER A NURSE, AS IN YOUR EXAMPLE, WOULD REQUIRE THAT SHE SPEND SIX HOURS A DAY OR MORE, FOR TWO OR THREE DAYS CONSECUTIVELY, WITHIN A FEW YARDS OF THIS HOUSE OR IN IT.

"The police weren't here that long."

IMPOSITION OF WHAT YOU CALL MENTAL CONTROL, AS ON THE POLICE, REQUIRES ONLY A FEW MINUTES. BUT IT

PRODUCES ONLY MENTAL CONFUSION AND SELECTIVE FORGETFULNESS IN THE SUBJECT AND IS USELESS FOR OBTAINING ACTIVE CO-OPERATION.

Studying the note Dan wondered how many plumbers, watermain ditchdiggers, gas company workers and unguessable others had labored at some routine job on the hilltop and then come away from it with vague feelings of confusion, unable to recall everything they had seen and done while working there. Now he remembered certain oddities in the angles and depths at which his basement waterpipes had been laid and the drains placed—all necessary, he saw now, if the earth under the oldest part of the house were to remain perfectly undisturbed. The enemy was no doubt telling him the truth now, but only part of it; it was not going to reveal all its powers to him unless it had to.

"And the machine?" he asked. "That thing down below that looks like a giant crab. What can that do?"

DO NOT COUNT ON USING THAT MACHINE IN YOUR PLAN TO OBTAIN SPECIMENS.

He got up and went to the cabinet and took another half-drink, straight from the bottle. He was ready to trade his right thumb for a cigarette. "Let me have a little more time to think."

YOU HAVE UNTIL TOMORROW MORNING TO PRESENT A PLAN. And then his limbs were taken from him, and the scraps of paper that held the enemy's messages, together with the marked newspaper, were taken up and stuffed into the bag of garbage that waited beneath the lid of its bright plastic holder beside the sink. Whether because of the greater knowledge it had just granted Dan, or the more extensive freedom he was perhaps to be allowed, or a new estimate of his intelligence, it was no longer taking him quite so lightly.

He was halfway through the preparation of a light dinner when the front doorbell chimed and control clamped down on him. His hand went to turn off the burner under the beans before he left the kitchen. Through the glass panels beside the front door he caught sight of the edge of Nancy's familiar handbag, and he experienced a feeling of heart stoppage that could not have been physiological because in fact his heart and lungs went working on in utter calm as his body walked to the door and opened it.

"Hi!" Her face was bright and innocent and smiling, anxious to see his.

"Hi!" Perhaps the slave-master too was capable of being briefly immobilized by surprise. It got out the one word and then just held Dan standing there, motionless inside the half-open door, looking at Nancy's Japanese eyes. At last it added: "Come in, Nancy." Perhaps the one brief syllable of her greeting had been enough to let it recognize her voice as that of the phone conversation.

She came in, already troubled by the change she obviously felt in him. She had an old suitcase in one hand—she had been moving in piecemeal, and never came emptyhanded. In the other hand she carried a small brown paper bag.

In the middle of the living room she stopped and turned, before even setting down her cargo anywhere, and asked: "How are you, Dan?"

"Getting along. Getting along all right, Nancy. Did you come here straight from work?" *No, no! Nancy, love, tell the damned thing that someone knows where you are . . .*

"Yes, of course." She held up her little paper

bag. "A couple of yo-yos for the kids. Danny, you don't look right, you don't sound right. How are you, really?"

"As I say, getting along."

She shook her head in brisk doubt and tossed the things she was carrying onto the sofa and came to Dan and put a questioning hand on his arm. Then her face tilted up and waited to be kissed. Of course the kiss was not right either.

She let go of him and stepped back with a long, troubled look. "How are the children?"

"All right. How are things at home?"

"With my folks? Oh, all right. I called Mom this afternoon. Dad has some kind of pain in his back. Maybe the moving was too much for him. But he went to work today anyway." A pause. "Dan, did you see a doctor yet?"

"Yes. Said it was only a virus, nothing to worry about." That line, Dan realized as soon as his lips had uttered it, was straight out of one of the afternoon's soap operas.

Even as he spoke his body turned away from her, and stood for a moment looking out of the window at her car parked just in front of the house, where the police car had been.

"I'm not going to stay very long tonight," she said behind him. "Promised mother I'd be a good girl and come right home as soon as I saw you were getting on all right." Her voice tried to be lighter. "She doesn't like me visiting a bachelor in his pad after dark, fiancee or not."

His fingers that had lifted the curtain let it drop back, and he turned. "Some day soon I think I'll drive in and pick you up." Was this from television again? Dan couldn't remember well enough to be sure. "We'll sneak out somewhere, just the two of us, like old times."

"Why, how romantic, sir." She smiled a little, but then continued giving him that worried look. She turned toward the kitchen. "I'll bet you haven't had your dinner. I'll fix you something. Where are the kids? It's getting dark."

"They're dining with some friends this evening."

"Oh! That's good, they're making friends out here so rapidly. Who are the people?"

"Just some neighbors."

She turned her back on the kitchen and came back to him, looking into his face more searchingly than ever. "Dan, it's me, you know, Nancy? I'm supposed to be moving in here in a few weeks, remember, like one of the family sort of?"

"I . . ." His hands took one of hers and held it, clumsily. "Nancy, I've just been going through a bad few days. Trust me, and things will work out all right." Straight from the soap operas again. Oh, if Nancy had come only a few hours ago, she would have *known* that something was hideously, vitally wrong, known it at once and without a doubt; but already the enemy was becoming damnably good in its portrayal.

She started to answer him sharply and then held back. Instead she asked: "When are the children coming home?"

He cleared his throat. "Later."

"Dan, what is it? What's the big mystery? Now I can *tell* that something's wrong. Did the doctor really say that it was just a simple virus?"

"Of course." The words came quickly and in a reassuring tone. Still the tone was not really, not quite, Dan's.

133

"Then what's wrong? Don't tell me there isn't something."

The enemy, being driven into a corner, only looked at Nancy steadily. She was going to have to find her own answer for her question, and of course she did.

"It's the children, isn't it, Dan? They don't want you to marry me."

He only looked at her.

"You got them out of here tonight when you thought I might come around. It's really that bad this time, huh?"

"Nancy, I think it may be best if you—don't see them for a few days."

Her eyes searched his, and evidently managed to find in them confirmation of her fear. But she was not despairing. "Dan, I can make the grade with them, really I can. Maybe I try too hard sometimes, bringing them yo-yos and stuff, presents every time I come. Maybe if I stop trying so hard . . . of course they're still going to remember their mother, and resent me sometimes. But I can live with that."

"You're a wonderful woman, Nancy." The actor's voice was gentle. "Nancy, will you just let me deal with things for a few days in my own way? Trust me?" Maybe life was in fact a soap opera, therefore the television dialogue all fit. "In a little while it'll all work out, I promise you." When Nancy started to drift again, in a slightly dazed way, toward the kitchen, he added: "I've eaten already, I was just cleaning up."

When she stopped, with a little shrug and a helpless half smile, he went to her and touched her cheek caressingly. "Look. What's today? Wednesday? Friday night I'm going to pick you up and we're going out somewhere, just the two of us."

She looked up at him, plainly wanting very much to be comforted. And she was; this kiss was much better than the first had been.

Nancy maintained her smile, and patted him briskly on the arms. "Danny, I'm going to start back, then. You can tell the kids it's safe to come home. Tell them I . . . well, handle it your way. You must know best."

"I'll handle it. Trust me, it's all going to work out."

As she was going out the front door, she said: "By the way, I gave your book to Dr. Baer."

"Oh?" The controlled voice was non-committal, mildly interested.

As they walked out onto the lawn, her eyes probed his. "The diary that you found up in the attic here, remember?"

"And what did Dr. Baer say?"

"I spoke to him again at lunch and he said he hadn't had a chance to look at it yet. He said perhaps by tomorrow."

Dan's body walked her to the Volks where it waited on their summer grass, and they kissed goodbye, and a few moments later she was gone, making a neat U-turn to get back to the highway. He was at once marched under control straight back to the kitchen, where his hand switched on the electric light and then picked up the pencil.

WHOSE WAS THE DIARY?

"I don't know whose it was, I hardly looked at the thing. I found it the day we were moving in, stuck away behind the chimney up there, buried in sawdust. I brought it right downstairs and gave it to Nancy, because she's interested in history . . .

but she doesn't have it any more, you heard her say that."

WHO IS DR. BAER?

"He's one of the curators at the Museum, in the city, where Nancy works. I don't know why she gave the book to him."

YOU WILL TELL ME ALL ABOUT THIS DIARY.

"It had a red cover. It wasn't very big. I . . . I told you I hardly looked inside it. There's nothing else I can tell."

He was brought to his feet so hard that the kitchen chair went over behind him with a crash. Marched into the first floor bathroom. Angry red burn mark right under the hot water faucet. Right hand brought across his body and held ready to turn the faucet on. Speech given back, but at whisper volume only.

"I don't know any more. I don't know. I did just barely look inside the book. Only a few pages had writing. There was a date, eighteen-fifty-something as I recall. The writing was hard to read, and I didn't care about it. I swear there's no more I can tell. No more."

After what seemed a long, long time, he was moved away from the sink, and, still under total control, back to the kitchen, where his hand wrote: THE BOX IN WHICH YOUR DAUGHTER LIES IS BEING OPENED NOW.

"What? Why?" He still could do no more than whisper his replies.

The hand went back and underlined the last two words of the next-to-last printed message. —THIS DIARY.

"I don't know any more. I've told you I don't know."

A muffled scream, in a high childish voice, came up from far below.

Dan's muscles would not lift him from his chair. He could do nothing but bring out his softened voice. "Stop it. I don't know, I don't know, I don't—"

THEY DO NOT SUFFER IN THE BOXES UNLESS WHAT YOU MAY CALL A SMALL GALVANIC CHARGE IS APPLIED TO A CERTAIN PART OF THE BRAIN.

"Stopstopstop. I'll do anything you say but I don't know any more about the diary."

A truck shifted gears going up Main. Someone drove by the house with rock music blaring from the car radio.

I WILL ACCEPT YOUR WORD FOR NOW. UNLESS YOU AGAIN FAIL DELIBERATELY TO HELP ME. YOU DID NOT TELL ME NANCY'S RACE.

"I won't fail again. I won't fail."

YOUR DAUGHTER MAY REST FOR NOW. IF IT IS NECESSARY TO PUNISH YOU AGAIN I WILL USE YOUR HANDS TO INFLICT PAIN ON HER. EAT NOW. BODY STRENGTH MUST BE MAINTAINED.

When control was released, he sat there in his chair like a string-cut puppet for a little while, even his eyelids sagging. Had to keep going, had to, had to. Millie and Sam. He was their only hope. Millie and Sam. Millie and Sam.

"I want to go out and get some cigarettes," he said into the air.

.CHAPTER.

10

On Wednesday night Dan Post suffered again through strange and terrible dreams. Dead Josie played the piano in the living room of the old house, and wrote in her red diary how much her living husband loved her still. On top of the piano, Nancy rested in her crystal coffin, and blunt-ended probes came out to burn her eyelids off. And somewhere Millie screamed. . . .

. . . as a small crowd of men in rough, homemade-looking clothes, with heavy boots, were gathering at night in the yard of a burning house atop a hill. With the setting of this scene the dream attained the familiar merciless clarity and control that the specimens' memories had when they came through to Dan.

The crowding men bulked over Dan, who seemed to be in a small boy's body once again, shutting him off from any clear view of the black-garbed shape that lay on the ground before the burning house. But when his host got in one quick glimpse between the men, Dan saw that it was only a dead man there, and therefore nothing very terrifying—not any more.

The men were standing stolidly about and talking, low-voiced.

"—Schwartz—" The name came through clearly from a nearby conversation, and Dan realized now who it was that lay there dead, and whose this burning hilltop house that stood where Dan's would later stand.

The men had firearms and pitchforks and torches in their hands to suit a vigilante task force on this warm summer night, but their talk, which had at first sounded like that of good humored successful hunters, was now fading rapidly into a morose silence.

Only the boy, Dan's host, seemed not directly affected by the spell settling over the group. But it quickly began to worry him, and he ran from man to man, looking up into their faces. Faces that would not see him. Eyes that would not focus.

Now their talk was starting up again, and scraps of it were clear to the boy's ears above the roaring crackle of the growing flames.

". . . both drownded like that . . ."

The men were turning to one another, animated once again, but sadly so.

". . . turr'ble thing . . ."

". . . both young'uns at one time like that . . ."

And young Peter, in whose body Dan dwelt again, ran in among them pushing and screaming: *Dad, Dad, Dad.* And the man he tried to cling to put him aside with a huge powerful hand, put him aside unseeingly as he might have brushed away a dog, and went on weeping, crying brokenly for Petey, his lost son.

The men standing about with their pitchforks and their rifles looked as foolishly dazed as two detectives were going to look in the living room of an old house more than a century later . . . and now the crab-machine came out unharmed from beneath the burning house. Knocking flaming boards casually out of its way, it scuttled straight for Peter. No mind control would be imposed on him, for him the collector had assigned a choicer role. He ran in terror, while none of the men who mourned could see or hear his screaming flight.

He ran at terror-speed but in a moment it had caught him from behind, and touched his back, and he went limp. Then from his fallen position he could see the crab turn and go back to Schwartz's body. It picked up Schwartz with two of its cable limbs, easy as a tiger hoisting a monkey, and threw the corpse toward the burning house, lightly disposing of a bit of trashy evidence. Schwartz's black-trousered legs flailed as he spun out of sight behind a curtain of orange flame.

"Reckon Schwartz's done for, too," a farmer mused. Spat at the inferno. "No way we could'a got 'im outta that in time."

"It's been a turr'ble week. Fust th' two boys drownded, then this."

"Wonder how t' fire started?" Then the speaker frowned at the torch he was carrying in his own right hand, and pitched it meaninglessly toward the burning house.

The men were beginning to drift away, Peter's father with the rest.

And now Peter could see, at the edge of the field

of his unfocussable vision, that now the crab was coming back for him. . . .

. . . and then Dan dreamed that he was Red, lying on the bank of the muddy stream with a steel needle in his back. . . .

. . . and all was going incoherent once again, and on the far bank savages riddled Nancy with their arrows, and black slaves caught her blood in great bark buckets, and Indians took it to anoint the great god crab-machine, demonic ruler of the universe. He saw it with a clarity as great as that of any of the previous visions, for just a moment: its feet shod in what looked like tanned wolf-paws, while naked brown-skinned men rubbed it down with stinking lard . . . then he was waking, while the crab seemed to call out to him some most profound, important secret, couched in the words of some language that he could not understand. . . .

And when he was awake, he would have chosen if he could to go back into nightmare.

When Nancy got in to see Dr. Baer, quite early Thursday morning, he took one good look at the expression on her face and got up from behind his littered desk and shut the office door she had forgotten to close, and then came back and led her to a chair.

"Now," he said, perching on his desk and hitching his right foot up over his left knee. "You want to tell old Uncle Conrad what this is all about?"

She had been crying very recently, and was near the point of tears again. "I want to know what you think of that book I gave you yesterday. Don't tell me that it's out of your field, please. It's out of everybody's field that I know. Just tell me what you think. I've tried to talk it over with my parents and my brother, and they all think *I'm* the crazy one."

Instead of whom? Baer wondered. He knitted bushy gray brows and reached behind him on the desk to pick up the red volume. "Well. Nice Spencerian handwriting, like my own Grandma's, before it goes to pieces toward the end. But I presume you mean the content."

Nancy nodded.

"Unless it should be some kind of a clever forgery, for what purpose I can't imagine, then I'd say the writer was probably suffering from delusions and hallucinations."

"Do you think it's a forgery?"

Baer smiled wryly. "Now I *do* have to say the question is out of my field—I can't tell whether the ink and paper is a hundred years old or maybe was made two years ago. The book doesn't *seem* especially old or worn. But if as you say it was dug out of some protected spot, I suppose that might account for its appearing new." He drew a deep breath and shifted his position. "One other possibility of explaining the content had occurred to me."

Nancy was wanly eager. "What?"

"It's rather far out, I suppose . . . but what if the anonymous lady was starting to write a novel, in diary form? Mary Shelley wrote *Frankenstein* sometime in the early nineteenth century, as I recall."

Nancy said: "The idea of nineteenth-century fiction hadn't occurred to me. But I don't see that it helps . . . besides, if it was only a novel, why hide it away like that?"

"Maybe the lady's friends would have considered novel-writing a vice. But Nancy, tell me if you will, why does it matter so much where this book came from? Your interest is obviously more than academic."

Now it was going to come out, and the words once started tended to be hurried. "You've met Dan, my fiancé."

"Yes, once, as I recall. On Members' Night. Seemed like a very nice fellow."

"Since last weekend when he moved into that old house, he's been showing symptoms very similar to those the diary writer attributes to her husband James. Talking about strange odors, having terrible dreams. And I went out to see him last evening, and he's not right."

"Not right? How?"

She made a gesture of not knowing; rather, of not being able to say just what she knew or how she knew it.

Looking at her, Baer was very serious now. "Has Dan seen the devil, too?"

Nancy gazed over his head. "We don't know that James ever claimed to see the devil, Dr. Baer. It was his wife who said *she* did. I haven't seen the devil out there either. I don't know what Dan's seen, or imagines he's seen. But I do know that something's terribly wrong."

"Well. When you say Dan wasn't right, do you mean he spoke—wildly? Or incoherently? Or—?"

"Crazily, you mean. I . . . don't know. I don't know. He looked at me at first as if he hardly knew me. Then he was too reticent, too uptight. As if he was hiding something. And he didn't want me to see the children—he must have sent them to some neighbor's house when he thought I might come around." She fell silent, looking inward.

"Nancy." Baer shifted around on his desk again. "Do the kids maybe object to getting a new Mommy?"

"Maybe . . . no, no maybe about it, they sometimes do. But that could be worked out. The longer I think about it, the more certain I am that there's something more wrong than that, far more wrong."

"Well then, is it possible maybe . . . I don't want to upset you any more, but bridegrooms do sometimes get cold feet before the marriage, you know, and . . ."

"You mean, does Dan just want out? He'd tell me, not act like this. If it was conscious. But maybe it's upset him. I think he loved his first wife very much. She's only been dead about a year and a half."

"Very well." Baer was frowning. "If he's behaving very oddly then I suggest it would be a good idea for him to see a doctor. I don't want to alarm you, but smelling strange odors that aren't there can be one symptom of a brain tumor. And there are other possibilities, I suppose."

"He told me that he had seen his doctor. But being a suspicious woman, I phoned the doctor's office just a few minutes ago, and when I told the girl I was Dan's fiancee she told me that he had made an appointment a couple of days ago and then phoned in yesterday to cancel out. He was evidently lying to me about that."

"Maybe he saw another doctor."

She shook her head, abstractedly, as if one doctor more or less would make no difference in a situation as grim as this.

"Nancy, Nancy, this is really tearing you up, isn't it?"

"It's no joke. He must have seen last night that I was really worried . . . maybe he is sick. In a way I almost hope so. That I could cope with. But . . ."

"There's more?"

Nancy nodded. "You see, he was talking about bad dreams, and complaining about these odors that came and went, from the first night he spent in the house, *before* he found the book at all. I guess I've told this badly. I must have given you the picture of him reading the book and brooding over it, and his mind ready to snap anyway with the strain of getting ready to marry me. Or something. But damn it, his mind *wasn't* ready to snap when he moved into that place. And he never had time to brood over the book, even if he were the brooding type, which he isn't, not ordinarily. I doubt if he even read much of it. Just brought it down from the attic and pushed it at me, saying 'Here, you're the history nut,' or some such thing—"

Baer's phone was ringing, and he picked up the receiver, listened a moment, then said: "Call me back, hey? About an hour?" He hung up and looked at Nancy. "Anything else?"

She nodded. "One point I've been trying to work up to. And the more I think about it, the more important I think it may be. A couple of times in the old house I had these—olfactory hallucinations, or whatever they should be called, too. Before Dan found the book, before I had any idea anything was wrong. Mine was woodsmoke. His was like something rotten—'rancid grease' is what he said."

Baer, who had started to get up from his desk, sat down on it again. "You had them too."

"Yes."

"Before you suspected he might be sick? Before he found the book?"

"Yes, definitely."

"Nancy." Dr. Baer walked around his desk to sit down in the chair, glanced irritably at some papers on the desk and then pushed them aside. "I'd like to hear this all once more from the beginning, if you don't mind."

Dan was in a sense relieved when Thursday morning's forecast on radio indicated that pleasant weather was to be expected for the next few days. Weather would be of some importance in the plan he had tentatively evolved, for securing what the enemy called a degenerate but preserved specimen for its vaults. He would really get it an old man or woman if he had to, anything to keep it from going after Nancy, anything to buy time in which he might find a way to strike back and set his children free.

After breakfast of cereal and juice and coffee in the sunless kitchen on the west side of the quiet house, he lowered his head as if he could look down through floor and concrete and earth to the machinery below.

"I want you to let Nancy alone," he announced. "That has to be part of the deal. Along with my kids being released, and me." Of his own volition he took up the pencil and held it ready in his hand.

The answer was not long in coming. NANCY WILL NOT BE COLLECTED IF YOU HAVE TOLD THE TRUTH ABOUT THE DIARY AND IF YOU CAN FURNISH ANOTHER SUITABLE SPECIMEN. IT IS NOW TIME FOR YOU TO PROPOSE YOUR PLAN.

The enemy's agreement was too ready to be at

all reassuring. Probably it didn't believe any of his promises, either; anyway he was sure that it wasn't going to stop watching him for a moment.

He lit his third or fourth cigarette from the pack that it had let him buy the night before, and began to talk. Explanation of his plan took a while, and then the enemy had some questions. When he had finished giving answers, the controller lettered one more word on the pad before him: PROCEED. And he was physically free.

In an attempt to show some willing loyalty he tore up on his own initiative the notes it had just written, and threw them into the garbage. Then he went up to Sam's bedroom and got out his son's Scout binoculars. Armed with these he stationed himself at the second floor window from which the nursing home, about a block and a half away, was most conveniently visible. He moved a chair near the window, and arranged the curtain so that he would not be too easily visible from outside.

He applied himself with patience, and saw that the good weather was producing the effect he had hoped for. By midmorning the nurses' aides (or practical nurses, or whatever their proper title was) were out four or five strong, supporting their tottery-legged wards by the arm on short walks into the mild sunshine, or pushing them in wheelchairs.

Only a block west of the nursing home, as Dan recalled, was a small park, and sure enough several of the white-uniformed girls were soon propelling oldsters in that direction. As Dan remembered, it was a small and quiet stroller's park, the big one with the playground and pool being some distance to the north.

Dressing to go into action, he looked himself over critically in his dresser mirror. Not quite handsome, but really not bad. No noticeable gray in the hair as yet, and the face showing only the interesting beginnings of lines. Before Josie, it had never been too hard to get to know the girls. And then after Josie . . . his eyes started to move toward Nancy's picture, which he had set upright now that her appearance was no longer a secret to be kept. But it would not be wise to start to think of her just now.

Should he put on a tie, or at least a sport coat? Then he would look like one of the suburban cops. He decided definitely against the tie, and at the last minute made up his mind to take a sport coat, at least carried over one arm as the day seemed to be getting warmer now. It added a touch of class.

The plan on which he had sold the enemy required that he persuade one of the girls who worked at the nursing home to spend enough time in his house for the enemy to establish physical control over her and make her into a puppet like Dan himself. Since this would require hours of work by the enemy, over a period of several days, it was not going to be enough to simply have her drop in for a cup of coffee.

In one variant of the plan, he would hire a girl as a part-time housekeeper; in another, considerably more personal appeal was going to be required. In either case, it wouldn't do for him to look like an utter slob.

Ready at last, freshly shaved and sharply dressed in a new sport shirt, knit slacks, summer shoes newly whitened, coat over his arm, he left the house on his own nerves and walked right along, going west along Benham as if he were on some decent business. He had left his front door half-locked again, just to appear consistent with what he had done before.

Mrs. Follett, working in her flower beds toward the rear of her large lot, looked up and answered Dan's wave with a gesture of her trowel.

"How are the children?" she called over.

He waited for a moment, expecting a clampdown of control that did not come. How are they, Mrs. Follett? Why as well as can be expected; they do not suffer unless what you may call a small galvanic force, in other words a voltage, is applied to a certain part of the brain.

No control clamped down, he realized with bleak despair, because with threats against his children it had found a better way. What could he yell to Mrs. Follett, while they were hostages?

"Fine!" he called back, his voice loud if not exactly hearty.

"You're looking better, too. How's Nancy?"

"Fine." He smiled and waved again, and walked on his way. Mrs. Follett, you tried once. You had the intelligence to call in the cops. What more can I expect?

He didn't know what more he had to hope for, but he was going to keep on hoping. Keep on stalling for time and piecing together whatever bits of information he could gather about the enemy. There had to be a weakness in it somewhere. Or he had to believe there was. Meanwhile he was taking a zig-zag course to the park, a block this way and a block that, still walking briskly along through the summer sun as if on decent business.

Once he had reached the park, and entered on a

149

gravel path that meandered through its shrubbery, he slowed down and began to stroll. He
breathed deeply of only moderately polluted air,
and turned his head to look at squirrels and birds.
Tall, broadleaved bushes gave the paths a feel of
privacy throughout much of their winding length.
Wheatfield Park was moderately famous for its lilacs, but it was too late in the season now for them
to be in bloom.

Here came the first of the white-garbed girls
whom he was going to encounter. This one was a
coffee-colored black, tall and almost modelish in
her posture, not at all bad looking. In fact she was
probably too good-looking for Dan's purposes. She
gazed straight through his effort at a friendly
smile and nod as she pushed along past him her
wheelchair with its blanket-wrapped patient. Perhaps she was absorbed in the mental images of
several boy friends who were already complicat-
ing her life unduly; perhaps she was simply contemptuous of this gray cat or white cat or
whatever offensive slang term she might want to
apply to him.

Too bad. Being seen around with a black girl
would certainly draw him more attention from
the world, and getting more attention seemed to
be one of the few things that might possibly help.

For the moment, he told himself yet once more,
just keep going. Something will turn up.

Here, only a few paces farther along the curving walk, came a second girl, a lanky near-
colorless blonde, pushing a white-haired and
white-stubbled old man in a wheelchair. Dan
played it a little easier this time. He smiled and
just barely nodded as he passed the girl, then
looked quickly away as if he were a trifle shy

himself. Before looking away he had just time to catch her answering smile of greeting, which was quite brief but seemingly unguarded. They both strolled on.

He took a side path that bypassed the black girl on the next lap of the sizable, roughly oval course, and then he made sure to intercept Blondie once again. "Beautiful day," he commented this time, smiling.

"For a change." Her voice was flat and unattractive. Smiling improved her face a little, though you still couldn't call it pretty.

He shot a tentatively friendly glance toward the wheelchair, but the old man seemed to be taking no notice of Dan or anything else in his immediate environment.

To the girl Dan said: "I suppose you're glad when you can get out of that place for a while." He had been often enough inside nursing homes, visiting Josie's late mother, to know what even the good ones tended to be like inside.

"God, yes." She stopped the chair, momentum transferring to the occupant's head, which began to nod gently and continuously as he continued to contemplate eternity, or maybe only the slightly browning grass beside the walk.

"Have a smoke?" Dan pulled the pack out of his shirt pocket and offered it, half-empty now.

"I shouldn't, but what the hell. Thanks." She accepted his match flame too. "Until you've worked in one of those places, you don't know what it's like."

"I can imagine."

"No you can't. Not until you work there." She started the chair moving again with a push that had something in it of the energy of anger, and

the patient's head responded as if with an agree-
ing nod of extra vehemence.

Dan faced about and walked beside her as she
pushed the chair. What did you used to say to
them, Dan? How did the old-timer in the story
put it? Heck, Bub, there just ain't no wrong way.

"You know, for just a minute there you reminded me of this girl I used to know, in California. I just had to stop and talk to you, see if you
were anything at all like her."

"Ha, I bet I'm not. You can't tell what people
are going to be like, not from how they look."

"You're really better looking than she was."

"Ha, that poor girl."

When they came to a bench she agreed, after
brief and formal protest, to stop and sit down and
talk for a minute. He told her his name. Her name
was Wanda Bartkowski, and she was sharing an
apartment with two other girls in a five-year-old
development in an unincorporated area not far
outside of Wheatfield Park. Her parents and one
brother still lived where Wanda had grown up, in
Cicero, well to the east.

"I live right over there," he said, pointing casually. "The one right on top of the hill." The
second-floor windows, open, were dark as empty
eyesockets against the white stucco but he supposed that no one except him, looking at the place,
was likely to be reminded of a skull. My God, my
God, he thought, how is it possible that I just sit
here talking calmly?

"So, do I still remind you of that girl?" Wanda
asked suddenly, breaking the short silence that
had fallen.

He tried to remember how he had decided that
girl was supposed to look. "As I said, you're better

looking. Nicer to talk to. You're taller . . ." What else? "Actually I can't remember her that well. Not any more."

"I ought to be getting back." But she didn't get up from the bench right away. She had a lot that she wanted to talk about with someone, and now that the process had started with mention of her Cicero home, it wasn't all that easy to stop.

While she talked, Dan kept waiting for some kind of opportunity to present his housekeeping proposition, but no good chance seemed to come along. So he just sat there looking at Wanda steadily and listening to her, giving his full attention to her every change of expression and her every word. It was one tactic that practically always worked with women, as he recalled. Whatever you wanted them to do.

What *she* wanted to do right now was talk about her life. For many years both her parents had held steady jobs, but now because of layoffs and health problems the family was in some economic trouble. Dan heard few details about that, but it was ominously in the background of all the rest. Wanda had dropped out of high school once, but then her parents had prevailed upon her to go back and finish. That was four years ago now. Then she had been either a singer in some kind of rock group, or some kind of camp-follower of it; that too was a little vague, but at one period she had been engaged to one of the musicians. It had never worked out.

Anyway it was all true what they said about the dope and the pot parties that went on among musicians; at least Wanda wanted Dan to believe that it was true, and that because it was, all that chapter of her life was now behind her.

"My parents said this was a nigger job, before I took it. But I wanted anything so I could move out of the house. I work with the blacks now and they're not so bad. There'd be more of them working here, but how can they get out from the city every day? Can't afford those commuter trains. It's not the black girls make it hell, it's the goddam patients who shit all over themselves, goddam them." She looked sharply at her charge in his wheelchair, but then relaxed again; it seemed plain that all the lines were down in that direction.

"You work nights somewhere?" she asked Dan, and then giggled briefly. "No, I guess you probably work in an office. Or you're a salesman."

"In an office, usually. I'm in engineering, in a desk-job kind of way. Just taking a few days off right now. A little personal trouble that I'm getting straightened out."

"You mean something to do with your wife?"

Right to the bullseye, hey? He had just one bad moment, and then found he could sail on in good shape. "Wife?" he smiled. "No wife any more. She's up and left, at my request. I'm selling the place as soon as I can get a buyer. Getting out of here and heading for California." He really didn't know why he kept bringing California into it. Just that for so many people the name seemed to hold the promise of some kind of heavenly glory.

"That's where your other girl friend was."

"I don't suppose she's there anymore. Say, what time do you get off work, Wanda?" Still keeping his steadily interested gaze upon her face.

She put on a slightly haughty look and looked

off into the bloomless lilacs. She wasn't going to answer that question for a stranger.

Not the first time he asked it, anyway.

When he parted with her, later, at the door of the nursing home, she left him with a small wave and a shy and suddenly attractive smile.

. CHAPTER .

11

"It's really very good of you to do all this," said Nancy, peering out of the right front window of Dr. Baer's Toronado, squinting into the declining sun to look for the house numbers on the suburban street. This was not as expensive a neighborhood as the one she and Dan had selected in Wheatfield Park; this was another suburb, farther west and south, and ran to old frame ranches, getting senile at the age of twenty or thirty and decaying respectably together.

"Now stop thanking me, you said it enough times already." Baer had put on his glasses to look for the numbers on his side as they slowly cruised along. The two of them had taken off early from work, Nancy leaving her own car in the Museum's lot, Baer growling: "Girl's getting married, people should expect her to take a lot of time off. Highest priority should be perpetuation of the species."

After hearing Nancy's whole story through a second time in his office, Baer had sat there drumming his fingers on his desk for a good minute and a half, his attention seemingly turned inward in utterly patient contemplation. "Nancy," he said then, "you realize that all these things you're telling me as facts, they just don't fit together as facts, in any one good explanation?"

She nodded almost meekly.

"Not even one good bad one, if you know what I mean. Not even any of the really tragic explanations of your mystery—Dan's got a brain tumor, Dan's plotting against you—forgive me—none of these will fit all of what you present to me as facts."

"You mean if Dan is crazy, or lying to me, or whatever, still doesn't explain why *I* had the hallucinations too."

"That's right."

"But there is one *logical* explanation, Dr. Baer. I don't say scientific."

"What is it?"

"That there may be something about that place, that house, that land, which brings this kind of experience on in people. At least in some people, sometimes. Buried chemicals. Maybe some kind of hallucinogenic gas, leaking up from underground."

He shook his head at that theory. But his finger-drumming started, very slowly, once again. "All right. Let us examine this hypothesis as logically as we can. Who owned the house before you did?"

* * *

"Should be right about here, Nancy, if we got the address right."

"There it is."

It was another modest frame ranch lost amid its peers, sided with green asbestos shingles, its white wood trim needing paint. Baer parked in front.

A thin, fortyish woman, whose half-tended graying brown hair made her look a decade older, came to the door in answer to Baer's buttonpush. Her eyes fastened at once on Nancy, who spoke first:

"Mrs. Stanton?"

Dan, having finished nearly a full day completely free of direct physical control, was surprised shortly after his modest Thursday dinner to feel control suddenly clamped down. His voice was left free, and as the master marched him toward the basement door, he questioned it: "What's up now? Something wrong?"

There being no pencil or paper within reach, it was perhaps not surprising that he got no answer. Down into the basement they went, through the tunnel and the heavy, click-sighing door, and down the surreal stair of slightly oily rods in the dry air.

The gimbaled table loomed before him at the bottom, the green lamps glowing on it brightly. Dan believed suddenly that the controller had suddenly changed its plans. Here I go, he thought, into my own glass case, and then we're off into space. There was something faintly tempting in the idea, the prospect of not having to struggle any more. . . .

But Dan's own body was not intended for the table, not just yet anyway, no more than Clareson had ended there. Dan's controlled hands now opened the cabinet in which the crab-machine reposed, and moved knowledgeably to lower it from its standing position so that all six legs were on the deck and bore its weight. It was at least as heavy as a man. Now his eyes were made to watch it critically as mechanical life came back to the crab, limb by cabled limb, and it quivered and stomped its ball-like feet and turned itself around. There was even a buzzing voice, produced somewhere inside the crab, that ran through what might have been a test-pattern of alien syllables. And Dan, his usefulness down here evidently over for the present, was turned around and started up the tilted stair.

Mrs. Stanton's sister and her brother-in-law, with whom she was still living, left her alone with her visitors in the living room as soon as a round of introductions had been completed. A couple of bats and a softball waited in a corner of the somewhat crowded room, but the children who had once intruded on Mrs. Follett's flowers were not in evidence at the moment.

"Miss Hermanek, what can I do for you?"

"I wanted to talk to you about the house, Mrs. Stanton."

The thin woman on the sofa showed no surprise, almost a sort of subdued eagerness. "What's happened?"

"I—I don't know that anything has. That is, I hardly know how to ask you about this, but . . ." Nancy's voice trailed off for the moment.

The woman on the sofa was slowly drawing up into a kind of stiff defensive posture, her arms folded. "You bought the house and the deal is closed. I have no responsibility in the matter." She glanced sharply at Baer. "Excuse me, sir, I didn't really catch your name. Are you Miss Hermanek's lawyer?"

"Dr. Baer. I am not her lawyer." He cleared his throat with a profundo rumble. "Actually I don't know what this would have to do with lawyers, Mrs. Stanton. I'm an archaeologist, interested in that mound the house is built on. There were just a few questions I wanted to ask you, if I may, in the interest of science."

"Science?" Mrs. Stanton blinked.

"Yes. For example, during the period that you lived there, did you notice anything unusual about the house?"

"Unusual." The thin woman seemed to be grimly marveling at the word.

"Yes, uh, for example, did you notice any unusual settling of the house? Any sort of movement of its foundations? Strange smells in the basement . . . anything like that?"

Mrs. Stanton had closed her eyes, and Baer and Nancy had a chance to exchange glances. Then they looked back at her intently. She was shaking her head a little, side-to-side.

"I don't know anything about the foundations of the house," Mrs. Stanton said. "All I know is that Richard was a well man when we moved into that house, and for about eighteen months thereafter, and six months after that he was dead by his own hand." She opened her eyes and stared at Nancy again. "For us it was a bad place. When you said you wanted to talk to me I thought that perhaps you people were having some kind of trouble too."

Baer put in: "May I ask, who owned the house before you did, Mrs. Stanton?"

"A family named Lind." Mrs. Stanton had no need to stop and think. "They lived there twenty-six years, and thought there was nothing wrong with the place, or so they claimed. Then the house was vacant for a short time before we bought it from them. After my husband died, I went and spoke to them as you are speaking to me now." Her eyes still picked at Nancy, and were now getting merciless about it. "There is something wrong now, isn't there?"

"Nothing *you* have to worry about, Mrs. Stanton," said Baer. "But before we get into that, may I ask how you first came to connect your husband's problems, that led to his death, with the house?"

The woman sighed. She thought about it, rubbing her bare arms as if they were cold, here in the cricket-chirping warmth of summer evening. "Well, I don't care if people think my ideas are foolish or not. I just don't care, not any more." She looked at both of them briefly, then off into space again. "My husband went violently insane before he shot himself, as I suppose the neighbors there may have told you. And I came to think the house was bad because it figured so prominently in the terrible dreams he had, when he first got sick."

When he and Nancy walked out again into the dimming evening, some fifteen minutes later, Baer roused himself from a preoccupied state to ask her whether she wanted to try phoning Dan.

"I feel like dashing over there, but I did tell him

I'd stay away for a few days. Yes, I want to call him. Let's get to a public phone."

They found a booth in a shopping-center drugstore, and pooled their change on the little metal shelf below the phone.

Dan's voice answered on the fourth ring. "Hello."

"It's me again, Danny. How are things going?"

"Nancy, how are you love? Things are going fine." And Baer, listening, felt the beginning of a frown displace his eyeglasses, even as his newly acquired half-belief in Nancy's theory was tilted also. The voice coming from the receiver sounded like nothing wrong at all. It traded banalities back and forth with Nancy, who nevertheless remained tense throughout the short conversation.

After she had hung up, Nancy was silent until she got back into the car with Baer. "I'm not going over there," she announced then, as if her companion had not heard it all with his own ears. "He says the children are all right. Also he broke off the tentative date that I thought we had for tomorrow night. Just wants me to bring the diary back the next time I come; whenever that's supposed to be—Saturday, I guess."

"Now suddenly he's interested in the diary." Baer had not yet started the car.

Nancy nodded.

Baer scratched his head, not knowing what to think. Shortly he said: "I'm going to take you home, but first let's get something to eat. Then tomorrow you and I will see this through to some conclusion."

"I'm really not hungry. Thanks anyway."

The engine broke into a thrum. "I know a place where you'll find something on the menu that will appeal. And we can talk. We have some talking yet to be done tonight."

They rode in silence for a while, out of the residential streets to a highway lined with electric signs. Then Baer asked: "What did you think of her story?"

"I was about to ask you the same question. It's practically my story too."

"Not so. Your man is still very much alive. But Stanton's having what sounds like the same dreams as Dan, and smelling strange odors too . . . I can't believe it's just coincidence."

"Then what?"

"Well, now I'm thinking things like, could there be paint with some poison in it, peeling or outgassing from the walls, giving some of the people who live inside those walls some strange delusions?"

"Dr. Baer. Paint peeling for more than a hundred and twenty years? And in between James and Mr. Stanton, a lot of people who were presumably never bothered by it all?"

"We don't know that there was no bothering in between the eighteen-fifties and the nineteen-seventies . . . but you are right, that's quite a span of time for anything like paint to remain chemically active, *I* would think. Hm. Lead poisoning? I wonder."

Nancy's attention had drifted away. "What? I'm sorry, Dr. Baer, I didn't quite. . . ."

"Never mind. Say, Nancy, my friends call me Conrad."

She was still off somewhere amongst her worries. "Dr. Baer, I think we should go to . . . to some authorities."

"Yes, but you see you hesitate to specify which

ones. But tomorrow we will decide that, tomorrow we'll take action. We'll go to see Dan, maybe in the late morning or afternoon. ... You know, damn it, Nancy, it still gets me that there may be an Indian mound under that house. Talk about coincidences. Adding another one like that would really be too much."

"It's just my idea that the house is on a mound. I'm no expert."

"Nor are you flighty enough to be seeing burial mounds everywhere when they ain't there. Not when you've got bigger worries. So *maybe*, I say, there is a mound. Not that I can begin to guess what possible connection it might have with our problem."

They dined, sparingly, at an excellent and expensive restaurant.

"I'm not coming to work tomorrow, Doctor—Conrad."

"Come in the morning, take a taxi or something. Your car is there, remember?"

"I can phone Susie for a ride, she lives up my way."

"Good. Because I would like to see a man there in the morning who really knows something about outgassings from the earth. And also a lady friend of mine who knows more about old books than you and I put together. Which I guess wouldn't necessarily be much, but she's pretty good. Then you and I will in the afternoon cut class once more, and drive out here and talk to Dan. Then if things look bad, we'll call in whatever help we need—if not so bad after all, then we'll just have come out so you can show me the mound. And we can give him back his book. Okay?"

"Okay." She reached across the table and seized him by the thumb and squeezed it quite ferociously. "Can I say thanks just once again?"

... it just seemed ultimately unfair, that the night should still bring him no rest, whose waking hours had turned completely into nightmare.

Dan knew full well, even as the Oriana-dream began again, that it was really a Thursday night in the thirty-sixth summer of his life, that he was in his own bed physically and that his body was asleep. But still he must experience the dream again, the same in every detail. It was as if he were strapped, with eyelids forced apart, before a wide screen on which this horror-documentary that he already knew by heart was beginning to unfold again.

Oriana dismounted with the others from the wagon, was led into the house, dozed first in the kitchen chair and then upon the floor. When again the crab-machine came for her (when Dan had uncrated it on Thursday afternoon, he had looked for any mark made by the heavy frying pan, and thought he found one, not a dent but a sharply polished spot half the size of the nail on his little finger), Dan's eyes through Oriana's were fixed again upon its waving limbs, its curiously shod feet. . . .

... and with a kind of electric snap the dream changed on him in a way that it had never done before. Now he knelt again in the medicine man's wiry body, which was quivering with what must be fear as his hands anointed the crab with stinking grease from his bark bucket, while before him in the roofless earthen pit the blue flames played over the convex monolith . . .

. . . snap again, and he was Peter, running in mad terror across the summer field, the breeze of his running cool on his wet skin, knowing that the metal beast must be in close pursuit. . . .

. . . and snap again, and Dan was wide awake, sitting up in his own rumpled bed, with somewhere outside the window shades the light of early dawn, grayness coming in enough to make a Rorschach blob of Nancy's pictured face at his bedside.

"But he wasn't caught," Dan said into the empty room. Peter had been naked when he fled the swimming hole, and now his body down below was clothed in shirt and overalls. It hadn't caught him until later, when the vigilantes had followed the crab's six-footed trail back to Schwartz's house and burned it down. . . .

Somehow Dan had always assumed that the dreams were sent by the enemy to torment him. But maybe not; maybe it didn't even know just what he dreamed. Maybe instead they were warnings, messages meant somehow to be helpful, sent to him from the other victims down below, from tortured minds that did not truly sleep, messages getting through the strange linkage that the enemy had made among them all.

Dan froze in his sitting position in his bed, his heart beating suddenly with the double adrenalin of hope and fear. Those four words he had just spoken aloud were echoing and re-echoing in his mind. He was afraid that his understanding of them had come too late to do him any good; and he was terrified that he had vocalized them for the enemy to hear. He sat there waiting for control to clamp down, for his life to be extinguished because now he knew the enemy's weakness and was too dangerous to be allowed to live. But maybe those spoken words had been too cryptic for an enemy who did not know what went on in his dreams. There was only the gradual brightening of the morning's light.

. CHAPTER .

12

Nancy's wristwatch indicated just three minutes after two, on Friday afternoon when Baer pulled his car up in front of the house on Benham Road. The morning's talks with experts at the Museum had provided a more-or-less expert opinion that the book was probably really a century or more old, but had been less helpful in offering support for the theory of noxious chemicals or natural gases.

The first thing Baer did on getting out of the car was to squint about him at the lay of the land. "I see what you mean about the mound," he muttered, nodding. "It just could be. But after grading, and housebuilding, and who knows what, on top of a few thousand years' erosion, there's really no way to tell without digging in. Anyway, we'll see."

He followed Nancy up the short walk to the low

little wooden porch, where she pushed at the doorbell and then peered in through the little glass panels beside the door.

No one answered. "Looked like his car's in the garage," Nancy murmured. They had seen as they drove up that the garage doors were shut.

Baer grunted, feeling suddenly, and really for the first time, somewhat sorry that he had gotten into all this. Maybe the young man was after all simply enjoying himself with another girl friend, human beings being what they were. Some appealing person like Nancy comes up with this intellectually beautiful puzzle, into which all known fact-pieces do not seem capable of fitting, and when listening to it one tends to forget that in the real world it is more than likely that some of the bits taken as fact are mistakes or lies or imagination. Nancy of course is an intelligent, reliable girl, but still. . . .

"I've got a key," she said with sudden decisiveness, opening her small shoulder bag. "I'm going in."

Baer said nothing, standing with hands behind his back. Unlocking the door, Nancy called in: "Hey! Anybody home?" When no answer came she went on in, stopping almost at once to shake her head at the living room's untidiness. Sofa pillows were disarranged and a corner of the rug turned up. She remained for a moment staring at a small suitcase and a small brown paper bag with its top twisted shut, that rested together among disturbed cushions in the middle of the sofa.

Baer hovered at the doorway, frowning uneasily, as Nancy took in these sights and then walked purposefully into another room. After being left alone in silence for a moment, Baer followed.

She was in the kitchen, which was in the same sort of casual mess as the front room. A couple of small spills, coffee or coke or something else brownish, had dried on the tile floor. The thought of blood, which turned brown when it dried, crossed Baer's mind. A plastic baseball bat lay in a corner, and a toy water pistol among the scattering of unwashed dishes beside the sink. A pad of notepaper and a pencil were on the Formica tabletop, as if someone had perhaps just been making out a grocery list. An ashtray holding several cigarette butts was there too.

"Maybe he's gone shopping," Baer offered.

"Maybe." Nancy stared down at the table. "Dan doesn't smoke."

No lipstick on the butts, thought Baer. But then a lot of girls don't wear that stuff these days. Why did he keep thinking there was another woman mixed into it? Just a feeling.

Nancy had left the kitchen and was now opening what must be the basement door. "Dan, are you down there? Children?"

No answer. She closed the door again and moved along. Baer followed her to the ascending stairs.

"Guess nobody's home, Nancy." He felt a growing uneasiness, not at what they might discover in the house, but at Dan's coming home and finding him, almost a total stranger, practically searching his bureau drawers. And Baer's wife, when he told her the story, would purse her lips and shake her head, I told you so, Mr. Smart Professor. . . .

"I guess not," Nancy agreed. But she went on upstairs anyway. Baer hesitated again but then trudged after her. Wouldn't want to be just standing in the living room, unrecognizable and undefended, when the householder came home. In the upstairs hall he came to a stop, looking with his neck bent backward at the trapdoor to the attic. He felt the pressure of the diary in his inner coat pocket.

"The children's rooms hardly looked lived in, even," Nancy fretted, coming out of what was evidently one of them. "I mean, they're lived in, but there's a kind of . . . of disused air about them. A little dust beginning to settle. Know what I mean?"

"Lived in, but disused? No, I don't know exactly."

She closed her eyes, thinking. "All right, I can be more accurate than that. A house with children is normally in constant turmoil. Toys and clothes and things are moved and broken and thrown around. Laundry piles up, walls and furniture get marked. Adults can leave a mess, too, but they tend to run in ruts, in tracks, unless they're deliberately being destructive. This house has—adult ruts. As if the kids have hardly lived here since the last time I saw them."

"I don't know . . ."

"And downstairs, that little brown paper bag on the sofa. In that are a couple of toys that I brought for the children when I was here two nights ago. It's still sitting there forgotten, beside the suitcase with some of my things in it."

Baer didn't know what to say in the way of reassurance, but he wasn't required to try as yet, because Nancy moved off down the hall abruptly to stop inside another doorway. "This was—this is going to be our room."

Following, Baer saw that the double bed had been slept in and was unmade. Mild disorder gen-

171

erally prevailed. A small click nearby made him turn his head sharply; it was only the digital clock-radio switching numerals. Two-fifteen. Nancy for a change had almost a smile on her face; he saw that she was gazing at her own picture, which was prominent at bedside.

"Well, Nancy, we could wait around for Dan to come home. Or, we could move on and come back a little later."

"Move on? Where would we go?"

He thought. "Do you know any of the neighbors at all? How about the lady who found the points?"

"Mrs. Follett, yes. I've scarcely met any of the others."

"Then I think we ought to go and see if Mrs. Follett is home. Talk about archaeology, if nothing else. Maybe we'll learn something."

She was too nervous to consider waiting around in the house. "I'll leave Dan a note," she said as they went quickly down the stairs.

"If you wish. You could say . . ." It seemed to be growing hotter in the old house, and coming down behind Nancy he lost the thread of his thought somewhere on the upper steps. He wiped at his forehead with his handkerchief. What was this bulge in his inside coat pocket? Oh yes, the red book, the . . . the diary.

"Say what?" she questioned vaguely, looking back at him from the bottom of the stairs, her eyes now as uncertain as he knew his must be.

"Let's get outside, Nancy, it's stifling in here."

Outside, she had taken three steps toward the car before she remembered to turn back and lock the front door of the house.

In the Toronado, he flipped on the airconditioning at once. "Better," he said, as the cool air came.

He looked at his watch again, with the feeling of reorienting himself after a nap. Only two-eighteen. "Now for Mrs. Follett. I deduce that must be her house right ahead."

"Right. Wow, that cool air does feel better. I was getting a little dizzy in the house."

Baer eased the car out into the road, and downhill a hundred feet or so before turning off onto the grassy shoulder again, to park under the shade of a large elm before the Folletts' house. Mr. Patrick Follett evidently saw them arrive, for he, graying and wiry, copy of *Time* in hand, met them at the door before they had a chance to ring a bell or knock. Behind him came Mrs. Follett, aproned, wiping her hands. The smell of something baking was in the air.

Mrs. Follett hugged Nancy as if she were a long-lost friend. "How are you, dear? And how are Dan and the children?" She led her visitors inside.

"I—I was hoping you could tell us something."

"Oh? Won't you sit down?"

"The truth is, I'm worried about Dan. Oh, I'm sorry. This is Dr. Baer, from the Museum. He drove me out today. He—he's interested in the projectile points, and also in the chance that our house may be on an Indian mound."

"How do you do." Baer shook hands with his hosts, studied them, and decided not to waste time pretending to talk science. "Nancy here is really concerned about her fiancé, and I admit I am getting that way too. Maybe there's nothing to worry about, but . . ."

Mrs. Follett was already nodding understandingly, for some reason not surprised at their worry. But she said, in hopeful tones: "I saw him

173

walking out yesterday afternoon, and he seemed well enough. Waved to me, but didn't stop to talk."

Nancy asked: "And the children?"

Mrs. Follett blinked. "Well, I understand that they were sent away to school. Dan told me that—let's see, on Wednesday morning."

"Wednesday?" Nancy sounded stupid.

"Yes."

"Away to school?" She took the chair she had been offered earlier, and Baer came to stand at her side.

"That's what Dan told me. Dear ... I hardly know how to say this, but for once I've really acted like the neighborhood busybody. I suppose I'd better tell you about it now."

Follett cleared his throat, and put a hand on his wife's shoulder. "Well, I don't know if you can say 'for once,' as if it were the absolute first time. But anyway, Nancy, Dr. Baer, you see I used to be associated with the sheriff's office in this county, and the police chief here and some of the boys are old buddies of mine. So maybe the wife and I call them up a little more casually than we would otherwise."

"What my husband is trying to say, dear, is that on Tuesday night I heard some sounds like ... well, like screaming, from over there, or so I thought. Patrick had fallen asleep on the sofa, and he sleeps like a log. Didn't hear anything. But then Wednesday morning I saw Dan, and he looked so ... so strange. I made Pat call the station, and later on in the day a couple of detectives came over and paid Dan a visit. They looked through the house and talked with him, and they were satisfied there's nothing wrong. The children had been sent away somewhere to school."

Nancy was shaking her head, stubbornly and with an expression on her face that looked like mounting horror. "Are you sure? I mean, did you actually talk, yourself, with the police after they went over there?"

Follett shook his head. "No, honey, Chief Wallace called me back. Said everything seemed okay. He's a good man, and I'm sure the men he sent were competent."

"But Dan told me Wednesday night that the children were having dinner at some neighbor's house." She could get no help from any of the faces looking at her. "What school were they supposed to have been sent to? Did the police say that?"

"I didn't ask them, honey," Follett said with the ghost of a chuckle. "Figured we'd stuck our noses in far enough."

Baer was looking toward the piano, where there stood the photos of a couple of grown-up young people. "Mrs. Follett, may I ask, are those your kids by any chance? Yes, well, then you've raised a couple of your own. You know how kids yell sometimes when they're being spanked or if they're just upset. Like they're being murdered."

"I understand what you're getting at, Dr. Baer. My husband suggested the same thing. But no, this didn't sound like any ordinary outburst. And then when I went over there next morning and saw Dan—I had found another arrowhead, and that gave me a pretext—he didn't seem at all himself. And he had these fresh scratches on his face." Mrs. Follett raised a hand to her own cheek, and Nancy nodded.

Mrs. Follett went on: "Now I've been trying to think where I saw the children last. I know they

were out there Tuesday evening, about dusk, playing in their yard . . . now come to think of it, isn't
that strange? I mean they must have been shipped
off to school that night, or very early Wednesday."

"Well, they could have been," her husband ar-
gued.

"But none of their suitcases are gone," said
Nancy in an almost forlorn voice. "And none of
their good clothes. If he did pack them off to a
boarding school somewhere to get them away
from . . . if he just packed them off, I don't know
what they took along to wear."

"Want me to give the Chief another call, young
lady?" Follett asked.

"No. I don't want to impose on you. But . . ."
She turned her head from side to side as if not
knowing which way to go.

Baer patted her shoulder. "Nancy, maybe you
and I will just drive over to the police station. This
may be a bit too complicated to go into it all over
the phone. Mr. Follett, I think maybe you *could* do
one more helpful thing if you would, give your
friend the chief one more call and tell him there's
two people coming to see him who are really not
as crazy as they may sound at first."

Follett agreed. "Let me see if he's in." He went
into the next room and got on the phone.

Nancy had a good grip on herself again by the
time she and Baer got back into his car, a little
after three o'clock. "Some things I've thought of,"
she began, in a businesslike voice. "Things we've
found out, rather. I don't know what they mean,
and I don't even have them in order of importance, probably, but I think we ought to list them
all, at least verbally."

"All right," said Baer, starting the car for the drive to the police station.

"Clue Number One," Nancy said. "The nonmissing suitcases and clothes; I can't believe the kids have really gone to boarding school. Clue Number Two, cigarette butts in the kitchen; if Dan's gone back to smoking, it's a bad sign. Clue Number Three, two different stories as to where the children are. I *know* he told me they were at a neighbor's." She opened her mouth as if to add more, but then was silent.

Clue Number Four, thought Baer, screams in the night and then the kids disappear and Dan has a scratched face. But he said only: "I'm looking forward to talking to the police who spoke with Dan. That should get us somewhere."

At the station they had to wait about fifteen minutes before getting in to see Chief Wallace. He was in his office, a small, windowless, but flawlessly airconditioned room with a few functional chairs, some metal bookcases, and a large desk as littered as Baer's own back at the Museum. The chief was a bulky man and beginning to go to fat, but he had a surprisingly sensitive-looking face, mild eyes that blinked at his visitors from behind mod steel-rimmed glasses.

He stood up as they came in. "Miss Hermanek, glad to meet you. Pat Follett says you're moving in next door to him."

"Yes," said Nancy, taking the front edge of a chair while Baer was introducing himself. Then, when all were seated, she went on: "I—I understand that two of your men have been to the house to talk to my fiancé. I've been trying to get Dan to talk to me, myself—I have the feeling there's something wrong, seriously wrong. I'd like to know what report your men made, if that's at all possible."

Chief Wallace cleared his throat and teetered in his chair; he appeared to be waiting to hear more.

Baer put in: "Let me state it plainly, chief. There is some doubt about Dan Post's health and sanity, about what he may have done with his children." He couldn't look at Nancy, not even from the corner of his eye.

"Are you a physician, Dr. Baer?"

"No sir, just here as a friend of the family. Of Nancy here. But what I hear of the young man's behavior suggests to me that there's some problem here that ought to be looked into."

The chief glanced down at papers on his desk and scratched his ear. "When Pat Follett called again today I got out the report on Post and looked at it again. It's very brief. Devenny and Harkins just say that they learned the children had been sent to school—"

Nancy broke in: "Where?"

The chief looked up at her over his glasses. "They don't say that, Miss." He bent his head again. "—and that they looked through the house and found nothing. Yes, I remember that struck me as odd the first time I glanced at it. Now they're both capable men, but that's not the way a report like this is usually worded. We want something more specific than just 'found nothing.'"

Nancy said: "Dan and I were planning to start the children in public school in September, here in Wheatfield Park. After we were married."

"Was there any discussion of sending them anywhere else? Boarding school, summer camp—?"

"A couple of camps were mentioned." It was a

reluctant admission. "But they wouldn't depart without baggage, and in the middle of the night. Mrs. Follett saw them playing Tuesday evening, and Wednesday morning they were gone."

Baer, watching and listening, could see Chief Wallace settling into the opinion that this was a nice young girl undergoing some conflict with her man, who was possibly not as much hers as she had thought. The chief had the report of his trusted men right in front of him, didn't he, saying, however vaguely, that there was nothing much wrong? Just as Baer himself had thought, off and on, up to an hour or so ago. But now Baer had been in the house himself. And there was . . . something. If he were a child, he might say that his mind still felt sore from that visit.

Hardly scientific, nor was it the sort of thing you told a cop.

Nancy had named the summer camps, and now Chief Wallace was smiling at her reassuringly. "Let's just see if we can do a little checking." He reached for his phone.

While the chief was waiting for his first call to go through, Baer suggested: "Assuming that the children are not findable at those camps, would there be any objection if Miss Hermanek and I talked to the two detectives ourselves?"

"No objection from me, except they're not on duty today. Harkins worked last night, and he's off now on a weekend trip to Wisconsin, won't be available until Monday. Devenny was taking his kid in to see the Cubs today, I think he said. Hello? Well, keep trying." This last was into the telephone.

As soon as he put the phone down it rang, but only to announce other problems. Accident on the

179

highway, and Nancy gathered that a man was killed. She thought of Dan, in spite of his recent calmness on the telephone, as wandering crazed somewhere, and her heart gave a couple of hollow thumps. But Chief Wallace while discussing the dead man on the phone did not look up at Nancy, nor did his expression change.

No sooner had he finished that call than another came in, something about finding an explanation for a delay in answering a burglary complaint last night. The beautiful suburbs, thought Baer.

He saw that Nancy was getting her nervous, restless look again. She was not looking too good at all, in fact, and Baer recalled that she had earlier refused lunch at the Museum.

He stood up and touched her arm. "Chief, we're going out to get something to eat if that's okay with you. Missed our lunch. Then we'll call back here and see what you've learned about the camps, and get Detective Devenny's address and phone number if that's okay with you."

Chief Wallace, phone still at ear, got halfway out of his seat to wave them good-bye. Baer got the idea that the Chief was not reluctant to see them go.

"Shall we check the house again, Nancy?"

"Yes, let's try."

A few minutes later Baer pulled the Toronado to a halt on the south side of Benham Road, opposite the house. Now the garage doors were open and Dan's car was gone. "Son of a gun. Maybe we just missed him."

"Yes." Nancy sounded fatalistically depressed.

Trying to keep a conversation going, Baer drove out to Main Street, turned south, and then west on Roosevelt Road, looking for a passable drive-in restaurant. While they were inside waiting for their orders to be brought to their booth, Nancy again tried calling Dan at home, with no result.

She had lost her impatience now, but gloomily, as if she were on the point of giving up. They took their time over sandwiches and coffee, and then Baer called Chief Wallace back and was given Devenny's home phone number, and also the information that the children were not at either of the summer camps whose names Nancy had given as possibilities.

Mrs. Devenny, when called, said that her husband wasn't home yet. No, she didn't know just when he would be there.

Five-fifteen. Baer in a cloud of rumination gazed out through the plate-glass window beside his front-booth seat, and nursed his second refill of coffee. Suddenly he saw amid the passing stream of eastbound traffic a face, man's face, leap out at him in unwonted familiarity. Beside the man rode a girl's face in dark sunglasses, trailing free hippie-length pale hair. The car was out of sight in a moment.

He turned to Nancy who sat lost in thought, staring at her fingers on the table. He asked: "What kind of car does Dan drive?"

She looked up sharply at the immediacy in his voice. "Tan Plymouth. Why?"

"Come on."

As they left the restaurant and got into his car he explained that he thought he had recognized Dan's face in traffic, quite possibly heading home. He said nothing about that other head that had been flying beside Dan's down the highway.

It was an anti-climax when they reached the

house on Benham to find Dan's car still gone and no one answering the door.

Baer tried to behave as if things were under control, problems being worked out one logical step at a time. "Well, we'll catch up with him sooner or later. Let's bother the Folletts once more. Maybe they've seen Dan, or maybe the police have turned up something and left a message for us there."

The Folletts hadn't seen Dan, though, nor could they pass on any messages, only the same friendly welcome as before, now maybe beginning to be just a little strained. But they offered the use of their phone and Nancy accepted, punching out Devenny's number.

Devenny on the wire sounded unenthusiastic, and a little slow, as if the trip to the ball game had been exhausting, or he had just been waked up from a nap: but when Chief Wallace's name was mentioned, he seemed to brighten.

"Sure, I guess you can come around and talk. Don't think I can tell you much, though." When assured that they were undoubtedly coming anyway, he asked where they were calling from, and gave directions.

Baer and Nancy had not much to say to each other on the way to the Devennys'. Not that an argument was building up, just that they had pretty well talked things out between them. Baer was now suspending judgment on the problem of Dan, holding his feelings a little back from events, as you learned to do when you got older and more scarred. What Nancy was feeling in her mood of quiet withdrawal he could only estimate, but he squeezed her hand hard as they moved up yet another front walk to yet another small suburban house. It was five minutes to six.

Devenny was young and very big. He took his callers into the living room while in the kitchen his small, shrill wife struggled to feed a pair of recalcitrant children whose father had filled them with garbage at that lousy game.

"Sure," the policeman said, when Baer had completed introductions and outlined their mission. "I remember the house, right next door to the Folletts'. Nothing wrong there."

"But where had the children gone?" Nancy was beginning to perk up again, getting her second wind. "I know your report said that they had been sent to school, but *where*?"

Devenny looked off into space. "The guy *must* have given us some evidence that they were in school, if that's what it says in the report."

Baer asked: "Surely he named some individual school or schools, didn't he? And then you must have checked up, to make sure the kids were really there?"

Shaking his head, Devenny looked a little sheepish. "Now it's slipped my mind just exactly what kind of evidence he offered. But you're right. It must have been something like that . . ."

"Did you look into all the rooms of the house while you were there?"

Devenny shook his head minutely. Surprised himself to find he didn't know. He was looking inward, as if at some phenomenon he found quite puzzling.

Baer pursued. "The children aren't registered in any school or camp that we can find out about. And there's no evidence that they took clothes or suitcases out of the house to go on a long trip.

183

Tuesday evening they were seen at the house, playing around, and early Wednesday morning they were gone."

Devenny was silent for what seemed to be a long time. "I just don't know," he said at last. "Don't know why, my memory's usually pretty good on this kind of thing. But the more I think about that whole scene in the house, the fuzzier it all seems."

. CHAPTER .

13

Wanda was off work early Friday. After a short stroll in the park and an early movie—rated R for raunchy, some godawful rendition of a worse best-seller, that bound itself somehow in Dan's mind with his real-life situation, so that he kept half-expecting the crab-machine to appear on screen— he bought Wanda burgers and beer at one of the classier drive-ins, after which they moved on to what the newspapers called a swinging singles bar.

The people Dan knew who had gone there called it nothing but Brother Bob's, which was what the imitation stained-glass sign at the highway's edge said. By seven PM the Friday night crowd was gathering in force, and Dan had to give up his stool to a strange young woman, as the sign above the bar enjoined all healthy males to do. He was drinking vodka martinis, and Wanda, gimlets. After two or three drinks he was definitely feeling the effects, though still very much in control. She was about a drink ahead of him by then, and getting somewhat giggly.

"Enough o' this, Wanda. I know a place where they got some real champagne."

"I don't like it. I tried it, and I don't."

"Not like this stuff if you haven't tried." He led her out of the noise and airconditioning into the warm night, toward his car round which a crowd of other cars had grown. So far the controller had been letting Dan do all the driving on his own. He hadn't been under direct control for more than twenty-four hours now, but he could take no comfort from that fact. The hell of it was, he had to admit that his adversary was judging his situation correctly; it had known just when it had him broken in and ready for dependable riding. Five thousand years or so of training and studying humans, breaking them to its will. What chance did one man have ... enough of that. Sam and Millie waited, in limbo or in hell, depending on him and no one else.

And there was no doubt that, even when he moved without control, the enemy was observing his every move. When he pulled out of Brother Bob's parking lot into the highway, which was still glary with the prolonged summer daylight, he could feel his master's touch upon his steering arm. It was a light and precise internal pressure that came and melted away again almost simultaneously, swerving the Plymouth gently away from a parked car that he had been about to miss by a perhaps dangerously small margin.

Along with other accomplishments, *it* was learning to drive. No, it had learned, with apparently superhuman speed and assurance. He would bet on it. The bleak thought came, not for the first time, that soon the enemy would know everything it had to know in order to function as Dan Post; and when that point was reached, he, his conscious mind, would somehow be turned off completely or else allowed to wither away under permanent control.

Again not for the first time, there came the savage impulse to end the unbearability of waiting for a chance, to act at any cost. To steer into that oncoming station wagon, for example. But he once more fought the impulse down. He would be able to help no one when he lay dead on the highway, unconscious in a hospital, confined somewhere in a padded cell until Monday when the psychiatrists could listen to his story. And the time for the departure of the collector of specimens was near. That was one statement of the enemy's that he found believable.

He would have to take the smallest real chance that came, but he could not grasp at any chance that was not real. And since the early morning when dreams had brought insight at last, he could believe a real chance was possible, in the house, where the enemy was physically present.

He turned the car off Benham onto the brief crackle of his cinder and gravel driveway, and eased into the garage.

A blond head lifted from his shoulder, where it had lately sagged. "Hey, this isn't my apartment. Doesn't look like th' fancy place I live in with all th' roaches runnin' between the walls an' dee-generates window-peekin' from my balcony."

"Wanda, l'il cutie, I'll take you back to all that marvelous stuff later. First we gotta have some of that California champagne I've been tellin' you about. Don't you remember?" He got out of the car and walked around to open her door, gallantly. She had started to open it for herself, but pantomimed joyful surprise at his gesture and let him finish it.

"Hey, you really goin' to California, are you?" she asked as she got out.

"Sure am." Slam the car door shut. "Soon's I sell the house. Wanna come along?"

"Aw, c'mon, don't give me that bullshit." She stood in front of him, not quite touching. "Your wife's comin' back tomorrow. Or next week. Or sometime. Right?"

"What wife? Told you, I got no wife any more. No wife at all." Standing beside the car in the beginning twilight of the cramped garage, he bent to kiss for the first time the slightly sour unfamiliarity of her lips, exciting in spite of the demonic watcher looking over his shoulder, and his own consciousness of unfaithfulness. He hadn't expected unfaithfulness in this would count for very much, not with the lives and deaths to be decided. Surprisingly, he found it still did count, enough to hurt.

Wanda resisted momentarily, but she was excited too. Once she had let herself be led along the walk and pulled into the darkening house, she clung to Dan like a drowning woman.

"Champagne!" Dan said, turning over and sitting up in bed. Since coming into the house they had turned on no lights, and night had fallen, but the window shades were still up and he could see reasonably well by the indirect light that reached into the bedroom from the shopping center's floods over on the other side of Main. Nancy's picture in the dimness was only a smeared blob.

As Dan sat up he disengaged himself from Wanda's bare body. His own body felt hollow now, squeezed and used like a throwaway tube. His mind was clear and free, poised on a knife-edge of alertness. He reached out a hand to fumble for his discarded clothing on a chair.

"Don' go away." Wanda's voice was drowsily peaceful. It came as a blurry mumble now because she was lying with her face half-buried in a pillow. She had been wearing a slip under her dress (to Dan's surprise; he had somehow gotten the impression that the young kids these days no longer bother with such impediments) and she was still wearing it, sort of, rolled up around her armpits. Now as he groped to get his shorts pulled on fly-frontwards, she raised herself enough to get the slip pulled down full-length again. Modesty, or warmth, or a birthmark she didn't want to show?

With his shorts on again—somehow he had felt guiltier with them off—he reached to get the cigarettes from his shirt pocket. "Smoke, Wanda?"

"I'm too sleepy."

He lit his own. In the candle-orange of the matchflame she looked incredibly young, and at the same time worn.

"Wanda."

"Hmf."

"I'm going downstairs to get us some champagne, baby. To toast our trip. We'll be on our way soon."

"I don't wanna go yet. I wanna stay here for a while." Her hand reached out to rest upon his leg.

"I mean our trip to California."

"Oh."

"I'll be right back, with the champagne."

He got up and located his white terrycloth robe in the closet and put it on. The robe made him feel somehow readier for action, and the feeling of being spied on, peeped at, was now very strong. Then he headed down the hallway for the stairs.

In the basement he had just selected one of the three bottles that lay in his plastic wine rack when a scraping sound behind him, from the direction of the tunnel, made him turn. He was bracing his nerves for another look at one of his hideously tormented children, but instead he found himself facing the crab-machine, which stood in the middle of the basement floor, motionless as a basking reptile. Dan saw that its six feet, which had earlier appeared to be hard metal balls, now softened and spread like clay beneath its weight, molding themselves to each variation of the rough concrete on which it stood.

The sightless-looking thing had one end of its body aimed at him. Now he heard again the buzzing rasp of its voice, coming from some invisible speaker, this time in coherent but toneless words: "The mind-signals of the woman upstairs indicate that she is sleeping. Do not waken her by bringing wine."

"All right, I won't waken her. I'll just get this bottle ready for later. You can get on with your job."

"My probing of her nervous system has already begun, and goes forward while she sleeps."

"But what brings you out now? I mean . . . why send out this machine?" Dan gestured with his champagne bottle toward the crab, which must be no more than a mobile unit running under remote control of some central electronic brain built into the ship below. The enemy had told him to expect no help from the crab in carrying out his plan to get a specimen.

No answer came. On impulse Dan started to move toward the tunnel.

"Stop!" The order buzzed at him sharply. The enemy in its metal body still faced him end-on, from about ten feet away. Now it had lifted its two front legs, something like a baseball catcher's half-extended arms waiting for the pitch.

He stopped. "I want to look at my children again."

"Their condition is unchanged. Go back upstairs and be prepared to entertain the woman, to keep her there, if she should awaken."

"All right." Obediently he headed for the stairs. Why wouldn't it let him go below and take a brief look at the kids?

Going up to the ground floor the crab stayed with him, moving a couple of paces behind like some well-trained dog. Why was he given this escort now? From above him in the quiet house there came a faint, soft moan, a sleeper's sound. Was Wanda entering on the Indian dream?

Bottle in hand, he entered the kitchen and headed for the sink. Why had the crab been brought into action *now*? What had changed?

Only one thing, that Dan knew about: the processing of another victim, Wanda, had begun. The suggestion was inescapable that while it was establishing control over her the enemy could no longer control Dan directly, perhaps could not even observe things through his senses. Its capabilities were limited. It was forced to put aside the Dan puppet for the time being, while it worked its controlling fingers into the Wanda. But it would still observe and guard him through the crab, and no doubt it could destroy him if it wanted to.

Standing at the sink now, champagne bottle in hand, he reached to turn on the cold water. He knew now that the time for action, the one chance, might be only minutes away.

Since waking this morning with new, dream-borne understanding, he had known what sort of action would be required. Thinking the matter over since then had confirmed his knowledge, as he saw how bits of evidence fell into place.

For one thing; why had the enemy's various slaves down through the millenia been forced to provide false feet for the crab? Tanned wolf-paws from the Indians, the hooves of cattle or pigs from Schwartz, bags of canvas or leather from Clareson. So that the crab would leave misleading tracks? But it was unlikely that any Indian or frontiersman would accept any sixlegged trail as being made by a normal animal. No, it had a simpler reason, according to Dan's new insight, for wanting to be shod. Its adaptable feet might be marvels of technology, but they had to be kept bone dry.

For another thing: why the roof of hammered copper sheeting above the vaulted tunnel? Not for decoration, it wouldn't ordinarily have been exposed. But as a shield against any rain or other water draining in, it would do a superb job and could be expected to last indefinitely.

And why the smell of grease down through the ages, unless it liked to keep its mobile unit coated with the stuff? Grease to do just what it did for ducks, keep water out. True, it had never asked

Dan for a grease job, but now the time of departure was near at hand. It didn't need shoes either.

And why, inside the specimen-collector's ship, was the air kept dry enough to hurt a human throat?

Even the medium that the enemy had chosen as a medium of torture might be a clue as to how it thought, in its so-subtly programmed unliving brain. It had chosen water. Had its makers' intelligence evolved, through some totally unearthly chemistry of life, upon a world where water did not exist, or existed only as a strange, corrosive liquid in the laboratory?

Water. Young Peter provided the clinching proof. He had not been caught by the enemy when he ran from the creek bank naked, because his body in its case was clothed, while Red's was not. Peter was not caught by a machine that had just shown itself able to move with the speed of a charging lion, but that had been unable or afraid (Dan drew much comfort from that word when he could fit it to the crab) to cross a small stream on the treacherous bridge made by a swaying log. Rather than take the chance of getting wet, it would let a specimen who'd seen it get away and try to spread the word . . .

Dan was now holding the champagne bottle under cold running water. Whatever move he made, he knew that he would get no second chance. He had seen in his dreams how fast the crab could move, how certainly it struck . . . it was waiting now twelve feet or more behind him, just inside the kitchen doorway. It seemed he could feel all of its electronic senses burning into his back.

It rasped at him softly: "Why are you doing that?"

"Champagne has to be chilled before you open it. This seemed like the fastest way." He had put the stopper in the sink, so it began to fill, and now he left the bottle in the water and went to the refrigerator, from which he extracted several trays of ice cubes for the bath.

The numbing conviction came that it *must* know by now that he had guessed its weakness, that he was getting ready to try to strike at it. As he carried the ice back to the sink he expected to feel the steel needles between his shoulder blades, or some other of the million fangs of death. But none came, and he kept on working with the ice and the bottle, and did the one other thing that he wanted to do, while behind him the crab still kept its cautious distance, well out of range of spashes accidental or otherwise. It would catch the heavy bottle if he tried to throw it, catch it softly and unbroken and fire back a dart at twice the speed. It would avoid the spray from the sink's hose attachment before the slow, low-pressure drops could fly that far . . .

He left the bottle chilling in the sink and neatly refilled the trays with water and carried them back to the refrigerator and put them into the freezer compartment at its top. As he turned back slowly toward the hallway, drying his empty hands on his terrycloth robe, the crab alertly scuttled backward from his advance, dry feet scuttering on vinyl and then on old wood flooring as they had upon dry rock and earth during the medicine-man's first grease-anointing of five thousand years ago. Had the Great Pyramids of Egypt yet been built when its long mission here began? And now in our years, the climax of that mission, as of so many other things, had come . . .

In the living room the crab stepped aside, alertly, to let Dan move ahead of it. He was half-way up the stairs, going to rejoin Wanda in the bedroom, when he heard bold feet, more than one pair of them, out on the front porch.

The machine, which had just been starting to follow him up, backed away from the foot of the stairs again as Dan turned to come back down. The door-chime sounded, cheerful *bing-bong*, followed without an interval by the crab's buzzing voice, pitched very low: "Do not answer."

He had been right, then, it couldn't put him back under direct physical control while it was still working on Wanda. The chime sounded again, almost before the enemy had issued its order. And then a third time, with no polite pause at all between. As it had sounded when the police came before. Whoever was out there now might well have seen his basement light go on and off, and they could see his car was in the garage. Let it not be Nancy, but no it couldn't be, at least not her alone, the feet had been too numerous on the porch.

The repeated chimings of the doorbell were joined by the fist that pounded on the door. Dan thought he heard a sleepy complaint voiced by Wanda up above.

"Remember your children," the voice beside him scraped, now even more softly than before. It came now from a little closer beside him, near the floor. The house was dim, but with streetlights and shopping-center lights, washing in through the unshaded windows, he could quite plainly see the tremoring cable-limbs, and the modest bulge on the smooth back. That was the high point on the low silhouette, the logical place for the senses to be located.

"They're what I'm thinking of," he whispered, below the pounding and the chiming, and thrust his hands into the pockets of his robe.

The battering on the door abruptly ceased. From upstairs a floorboard creaked; Wanda must be up, wondering what was going on. Out on the porch, a man's low voice rumbled something, ending with: ". . . warrant."

A woman's voice replied with a few words, again only the last of them being plainly audible to Dan: ". . . key."

Surely the people out on the porch must be able to hear his heart. The metal beast that stood beside him turned to face the door, and something in its body clicked, and a dark stubby nozzle was suddenly visible projecting from the center of its hump toward the door. The sound was answered on the instant by another click, this one from the front door's lock, as a key was scraped in to set its tumblers and the bolt shot back.

Dan's right hand came out of the pocket of his robe, holding Sam's water pistol which he had picked up and loaded at the sink. In the same motion he aimed as best he could, and squeezed off the pistol's soundless stream at a range of about five feet against the enemy's unliving back.

It was as if he sent live steam against a living nerve. Quick as a flea for all its mass, the crab leaped clear of the floor, going as high as Dan's head into the air. As it twisted in midair convulsively, one of its outflung limbs caught at the collar of Dan's robe. Whether it had intended a grab at him or not, he was jerked forward so violently that he left his feet.

Even as he flew, he cried out a wordless warning to the people at the door. And even before he hit the floor, he felt the full power of the enemy's direct interior control crack down on all his muscles, with a force that must be meant to kill.

In the same moment Wanda screamed loudly from upstairs, and the vise of control left Dan as quickly as it had come, before it could do him injury; the enemy must still be psychically entangled with her nervous system. And simultaneously the crab came down from its own agonized leap, hitting the wood floor like a falling safe.

The momentary seizure of control had cost Dan his water pistol, which was lost somewhere on the floor. He did not stop to look for it, but came out of his somersault into a crouch, and ran crouching for the kitchen, ran like a sprinter getting off the blocks, for the sink filled with cold water, for the bottle to be thrown like a grenade. Upstairs, Wanda screamed again, and for the time being Dan was free.

Even as he crossed the living room, the front door was swinging wide; and from the corner of his eye Dan caught sight of a man crouched there with what appeared to be a pistol in his hand.

The collector's remote-control unit was struggling to regain its coordination. Its electronic nerves were still shocked and partially incapacitated by drops of the corrosive liquid that had been sprayed along its skin, that had run in around its laser nozzle through seals and grommets rusted and weakened by agelong exposure to this deadly, watery atmosphere. It was unable to react in time to prevent the potential specimen Dan Post from getting out of the room. Though it swiveled its laser and sent one burst of destructive energy after him, its aim was still affected by the water; and by the time it adjusted its aim Dan was out of sight. The ray missed its moving target.

Part of the wall beside the entrance to the kitchen exploded into flames as the fragile-looking pencil of light struck home. The color of the beam changed from red to blue to green and back again, in a rapid randoming designed to prevent effective defense by reflection; and the interior of the house was lighted up by it in a rapid strobe effect.

The collector through its mobile unit saw that men at the front door, taking shelter behind the woodwork at each side, had now drawn weapons and were starting to take aim. The collector recognized the weapons as handguns of some kind, and thought it likely that great technological progress had taken place in this field in the century and more since it had last been able to examine the native firearms. Therefore it could not afford to ignore the threat those handguns represented, and it turned its laser against the police at once.

The mobile unit's aim was still slightly erratic, as its circuits struggled to recover from the shock of the destructive water. Again flames leaped from the wall, this time on either side of the doorway; and the fragile-looking beam lanced out into the night, straight and thin as a draftsman's line. A gray-haired man standing awkwardly in the middle of the walk went down, and a treetop a block south of Benham Road burst into fire.

Less than a full second later, both policemen at the sides of the open door were firing back, and the collector realized that its wariness of their weapons had been unnecessary. The guns were only projectile-throwers not essentially different from those of a century before, devices that used the force of exploding chemicals to send bits of heavy metal spinning outward at no more than a few hundred meters per second; those bullets which were aimed accurately struck without damage to the remote-control unit's outer surface, which had been designed to withstand any weapons that the designers could imagine primitive life-forms being able to employ.

But how could the designers, in the dry chemistry of their silicon brains, ever have imagined that any kind of life, let alone intelligence, could flourish on a world where solids and liquids and gases alike were rich in water?

The potential specimen Dan Post had come to understand the collector's vulnerability, evidently, and was in the kitchen now grabbing a container, a plastic bowl, and starting to fill it at the sink. The collector made the mobile unit lurch forward two strides on its still-unsteady legs, and threw another laser bolt toward the kitchen. Almost beneath Dan's fingers, the sink and its faucets and its champagne bottle and its piping burst into fragments of hot metal and glass and a charge of steam. Small droplets of molten metal and scalding water struck at his robe and at his hands and face, and he was weaponless again and for a moment he thought his eyes were gone. He lurched to the kitchen door and staggered out into the night.

The collector also moved its mobile unit toward the open air, avoiding the continuing spray of water and steam from half-melted plumbing in the kitchen. It stepped toward the front door, its coordination gradually recovering from the water-pistol spray, legs regaining their sureness of movement. In a hundred years and more the grease of its last protective coating had hardened and flaked away, and droplets of the stinging water now continued to cling like attacking insects to its ceramic-metal skin, each droplet perceived by the sensors beneath as a tiny, biting, destructive mouth. Fortunately for the collector, the mobile unit's internally generated heat was already driving the moisture away by evaporation; a dose of two or three times as much, as well-aimed at the sensitive joint between laser nozzle and body, might well have permanently crippled the mobile unit or caused its total failure.

The men on the porch were continuing to fire their guns, and the collector fired back again, wanting to eliminate them before they could come up with more effective weapons or call in help. The wooden walls between still saved the men from the laser's full direct force, and one of them was able to run halfway back to their vehicle at roadside before he fell. The other man was still alive and screaming when the mobile unit reached what was left of the burning doorway, and the man pounded at the unit's hard surface with his empty handgun until it wrapped a limb about him and threw him some distance out into the yard. Specimens on this planet were thin-skinned bags of watery fluids, dangerous to handle when burst or leaking.

In the flame-rimmed doorway the collector brought the mobile unit to a halt, letting the heat of the surrounding fire boil out what remained of the corroding water from inside the joinings of its armor. Meanwhile the collector turned its full attention to the starship into which it had been built. Of course it had already abandoned its work toward controlling the female potential slave, who still lay upstairs, half-conscious from its psychic violence. Now for a few seconds it was busy issuing electronic orders to tens of thousand of components, testing a hundred systems, beginning at emergency speed the preparations that must be made to get the ship out of the earth and start the long voyage home. Only minutes would be needed for the ship to dig itself out of its age-long concealment and start the climb for space, on engines that would leave behind a megaton's worth of death by radiation.

Then the collector transferred its attention back to the mobile unit, and walked it out into the world. Now that all hope of remaining in concealment was gone, it could act quite openly, and its valuable last few minutes upon this planet should not be wasted. There was still room for two more human specimens inside the ship. As it crossed the porch, the sensors of the mobile unit felt the first preliminary lurching of the ground beneath its feet, meaning that the ship below was getting ready to come up.

Some fifty meters down the hill there was a rapid movement among tall flowers and bushes, and then a crash as a human body flung itself through the glass of flimsy doors and vanished into the nearest house in that direction. The human called Dan Post, no doubt; the collector once more threw a beam of fire, and though it thought it did some damage its aiming circuits were not wholly recovered from the water, and once more it had to estimate that it had failed to kill. More trees and bush flared into flame, and along the side of the Folletts' house some masonry splashed into gobs of lava. To re-establish direct control over the escaping slave would now take some time, for the collector's control circuits were in disarray, half of them still set up to explore the female's nervous system; and the collector did not want to take the time, because Dan Post was not the type of specimen it sought, and the mobile unit could now gather others far more effectively than his controlled body could.

The collector's attention was drawn by a movement inside the police vehicle parked at the edge of the road. Door slamming and a rising barrier of window glass, and the face of a woman looking out from the front seat, a face in which the epicanthic eyefolds were plainly visible, the face called Nancy.

The most desirable specimen was right at hand.

Her key had turned in the lock and she had pushed the door open, standing between Chief Wallace and Devenny, with Baer looking over her shoulder. Then Nancy had started back instinctively from the scuffle and violent motion that exploded in the darkened interior of the house. She heard Dan's wordless yell, but was not sure it came from him. Then the needles of violent fire came stabbing from somewhere in the living room, striking new flames from everything they touched. In terror then Nancy fell back farther, and when she saw most of Dr. Baer's head go off in a great cauterizing blur of light, she turned and ran for the police car on the street.

Against the background of noise and flames, flares and explosions and gunshots, the conviction was somehow establishing itself in her mind that Dan was dead already. She did not see him flee the house. But Nancy's mental state was not disabling panic, she still functioned. She picked up the microphone of the car's radio and worked it as she had seen the policeman work it earlier.

"This is an emergency," she reported, keying the button for transmission, her voice calm and almost lifeless with shock. "Car One reporting. People are being killed at three-twenty-six Benham Road. There's a big fire, too."

And now the woman of the diary came into her mind, for Nancy had just this moment seen the devil come out onto her porch, framed by the hell-flames from what had been the doorway of her house.

A male voice on the radio was starting to demand that she identify herself, and she overrode it calmly. "This is not a hoax. If you look out your window you can see the fire, it's on the highest point in town."

Then she let the microphone fall from her hand, for she realized that the devil in the shape of a giant crab or insect was coming straight for her, having thrown the fallen bodies of the two policemen out of its way. A limping, slightly drunken devil whose six legs scraped and tremored at the grass uncertainly, but it was coming toward her all the same. She found that she had already raised the window and locked the car door, and now she slid into the driver's seat.

Even as she turned the key in the ignition, fingers moving with what in her terror seemed fatal slowness, she felt a certain paradoxical happiness. Whatever devil it was, it was not Dan. He might be dead, but he had not willingly deserted her.

The engine roared into life just as the menacing shape reared up outside the window to her right. Something smashed in through that window's shatterproof glass even as Nancy's foot found the accelerator and her fingers slid the selector lever into drive. One glance to her right as the car began to move showed her a metallic-looking cable or arm come reaching in, groping on the right-hand door for the button that would release its lock and let it be opened from outside.

The powerful police car shot west on Benham, gathering speed, just as something inside the door gave way with a snapping of metal that testified to the force applied. The devil had not found the lock release and was not going to bother with it. Before the auto had gone a hundred feet, Nancy had the impression first that the glass was being ripped out of the right front door, and then that the whole door was going. Then something like a steel cable with a bright metal ball at the end came in front of her. With the amazing dexterity of an elephant's trunk, it snatched the ignition key from its socket, then took hold of the steering wheel and effortlessly overcame her own grip with a hard twist to the right.

There had not been time for the car to build up speed enough to make it roll with the tight right turn, but wheels screeched as it jolted up onto the grassy shoulder of the road and then across the Folletts' lawn. Nancy threw her own door open and moved instinctively to jump, the centrifugal force of the turn adding momentum to her movement. She felt a steel-hard arm tear at her clothing as she fell free.

The grass came up to hit her, and momentum whipped her through an easy somersault. She came upright to see the police car jouncing into a small tree that bent down unbroken under the vehicle and brought it to a stop. Some shape that was not human was moving in the driver's seat . . .

"Nancy! This way!" The voice coming from behind her was Dan's, and she turned to see him, a specter in a bloodied, dirty white bathrobe, framed in the shattered French windows of the Folletts' house, with their faces gaping whitely on either side of his, all of them plainly visible in the light of the burning house atop the hill.

In a moment Nancy was on her feet again and running toward them, moving in a high-speed limp with one of her sandals gone somewhere. Flames roared behind her in the night, and in the distance people shouted.

Dan vanished again from the darkened cave of the French windows, now only a dozen strides ahead of Nancy, but now Patrick Follett's lean figure stood there in pajamas. He had a revolver in his hand, and was shooting at something behind Nancy. The expression on Follett's face was one of comically exaggerated horror.

Had Dan really been there at all? Nancy took two more limping, running strides, and then felt the gentle touch between her shoulder blades. Immediately she went down, the neat short Follett grassblades whipping at her face as she rolled over once more on the lawn. Her voluntary muscles were suddenly useless, though her nerves were still awake to all sensation.

The rolling fall left her with her face turned back toward the east. The house on the hill was now beginning a slow collapse into flaming ruins, even as great cracks spread around it through the earth. As Nancy watched in utter helplessness, there ran from the house a human figure dressed in white and trailing smoke. The figure collapsed on the lawn just outside the house, even as a good part of the building came down in an avalanche of crackling stucco and breaking wood. And now the earth-cracks grew and spread, as if the age-old mound beneath the house were no more than an egg, some great roc's egg that now was breaking rapidly and just about to hatch . . .

The collector's mobile unit had now fully shaken off the effects of the water-pistol spray, and was now proceeding methodically from the stopped car to pick up the paralyzed specimen designated Nancy. The collector meant to put her aboard the ship, as soon as the entrance hatch had come conveniently above ground. Then, the collector calculated, there would probably still be time to send the mobile unit after one more specimen, one of the aged-but-preserved type to round out the collection. Then it would be desirable to take off quickly, and begin at once the long voyage home. The dominant race of this planet now had technological capabilities that would be dangerous if they could once be brought to bear on the invader.

The remote-control unit reached the still body of the immobilized female, and reached with two cable-like limbs to pick her up. And all around it the lawn erupted with a hundred acid jets of water.

Dan, with his one usable hand gripping the valve of the Follett's lawn-sprinkler system, saw the machine jump and twist in mid-air again.

This time the convulsion did not cease after a single spasm. As soon as the heavy body fell to earth, nearly on top of Nancy, it was immediately flipped into the air again by the wild thrashing of its limbs. The assault of the sprinklers continued against the crab, a thousand tiny sprays that drenched every square inch of its body.

The collector could no longer use it purposefully against Nancy, but in its convulsions it threatened to fall on her and break some bones by accident. Dan left his place at the valve, and ran out of the Folletts' house. Follett and his wife came with him, Patrick now having discarded his revolver. It took all of them to gather up Nancy's dead weight and carry her inside; Dan's left arm was wounded and useless, since the enemy's last laser shot at him.

There was the dart, steely and blunt and pressed somehow against Nancy's back, right over her spine.

Follett was looking at her face. "I'm afraid she's gone, Dan."

"No. Get her to a hospital, will you? I've seen this before. She's just paralyzed. That dart'll have to be removed, how I don't know. Now I've got to go after my kids."

"Wait, Dan, your arm—" Mrs. Follett tried to hold him, but he was outside again, running barefoot uphill toward the tottering, falling, flaming ruins of his house. In his front yard a human voice was crying out in pain, and he got his good arm around a burned woman wearing a torn white slip, and pulled her farther from the flames.

With a wild howling of sirens, fire engines were converging on the hill from east and west at once, their searchlights sweeping the battlefield that had been Dan's and Nancy's yard. Simultaneously with their arrival, what was left of the house shuddered and came down. But already something else stood where it had been, something that reared itself out of the soil on girder-like metal arms, grew taller as the house had been, like some mad giant robot swimmer surfacing.

But the collector had not yet got its starship free. Spray from broken water pipes ate and burned at the ship's hull, and the flat bluish coat of flame that Dan remembered from the Indian dream now sprang out over the entire visible surface.

"Get water on that thing! Water!" Dan yelled as he ran to meet the charging arrival of the firemen from the trucks. Men wearing sloping hats and rubber coats surrounded him, glanced at his blood and wounds—things they had seen often enough before—and then gaped behind him at the blue blazing thing that pulled itself up out of the earth.

"Get water on it—hoses—quick. My kids are in that thing. It killed these men—" Motion about him at the bodies scattered in his yard. Now more police were on the scene, more guns drawn. Nowhere to shoot. Dragging at the body of their chief.

"Water!"

Somehow he was heeded. Firemen with tools were twisting at the hydrant across the street. Flat hoses stirred and bulged, becoming angry snakes.

"Water! Goddamn you, can't you hurry? That fire's not electrical." Not giving a damn whether it was or not.

The enemy had no laser now, or it could not get another into use in time. No lance of flame to fight back with. Its fighting unit twitched and slowly melted, like hard sugar, in the persistent sprinklers some forty meters down the hill . . .

Men were aiming the nozzles of the ready hoses now. Armed with the fluid of life, the blood of Earth, from which all men and microbes sprang. . . .

The enemy ship was almost free before the crystal lances of the firemen struck out. The blue flames, hopelessly inadequate defense against this kind of an assault, were splashed aside, were quenched like candles so only the firetrucks' searchlights now held away the dark.

Dan clutched at unknown shoulders frantically. "On that hatch there! See? That door! Aim your hoses there."

The hatch resisted for a while, as the ship kept trying to get upright for a launch. Its tree-sized limbs flailed and shivered as the earth that held its weight now turned to mud. And now the outer layers of the hull itself were beginning to melt and slide like foggy earth. The hatch fell open suddenly, the streams from hoses went pounding triumphantly inside.

The crystal caskets, fabricated somehow to contain the watery life of this strange and watery planet, were among the few parts of the ship that would not rapidly corrode and melt when wetted down. The caskets had to be forced open with the firemen's crowbars and axes. Millie's case was the first one to be broken into, and Dan used one of the steel bars himself. She murmured "Daddy" and held up her arms as soon as she had pulled her out.

▪ CHAPTER ▪

14

They were riding toward the tallest office building in the world, with a dim moon not far above it in the sky, a bluish moon just hinting at what lay beyond. The big car, going deep into the city, swooped along the expressway, now rising over a cross-highway, now plunging into an underpass. Dan and Nancy, and the television reporter they had come to like during their week of sudden fame, were riding in the back seat of the sedan, and the government driver and the other government man, the important one, were up in front.

Dan's left arm was still bandaged and he carried it in a sling, and his face and hands still bore small burn marks. But his wounds were a week old now and the pain was no longer continuous. Nancy's whole body had been stiff for a couple of days after the doctors had taken a chance and forcibly pried the peculiar needle away from her spine, but the stiffness was gone now, and she seemed to be suffering no other aftereffects.

Sunset was coming on, and the windows of the towers ahead now glittered orange with its reflection.

"Dan," the reporter was saying, in his voice that any experienced television-watcher in the nation could have imitated, "There has been a suggestion made about which I'd like to have your personal feelings. Some scientists have suggested that there may be other interstellar probes, similar to the one you encountered, on the earth right now, sent by the same civilization that sent yours. It would seem that such probes could have found drier environments than Illinois, certainly, places in which their chances of survival should have been much better."

"You want to know what my feelings are?" Dan's voice was low and even, and he was staring straight ahead. "All right. I think that there are other probes. I don't believe I'll ever walk into a house again without wanting the basement checked out first." He was not smiling, not a trace. Nancy stroked his good arm.

He went on: "I don't know where I'm going where I'm going to be able to live the rest of my life. Nancy's father has suggested Key West. He was stationed there in the Navy. Humid, surrounded by ocean, and he tells me that if you dig down two feet you hit salt water."

The white-haired man in the right front seat— not just a government man in the usual sense, but the adviser of a couple of presidents—turned and said: "Dan, if you and Nancy should seriously want something like that arranged, we can do it,"

"You've done a lot already, thanks," said Nancy.

Dan said: "Present quarters in the hotel are fine for now. After the wedding . . . well, we'll have to talk it over." His eyes held Nancy's for a while.

The reporter asked: "How are the kids doing today?"

"They seem to be coming along," said Nancy. "Our two at least."

"No sedation of any kind for the past twenty-four hours," Dan amplified. "The doctors say their reactions now seem almost normal—I think so too. Of course, I expect there'll be some mental scars remaining." He paused, and shook his head. "And then there's Pete, and Red. I feel almost like a relative, after living through that business with them. I want to take an interest in their future. And Oriana's too. They're all coming around, though more slowly than my guys. And even the Indians are all still alive. At least they're breathing again, though some of them were in that thing five thousand years. Beginning with the Middle Archaic Culture . . . well, Nancy can tell you about that."

They were leaving the expressway now, ascending a long cloverleaf curve that brought them into a city neighborhood whose wide streets appeared to be lined chiefly with hospitals and parking lots. Most of the buildings were aging and somewhat grimy, though here and there appeared new steel and glass. Almost all of the visible pedestrians were black. Cars were parked bumper-to-bumper along most of the curbs, and traffic was slow and quiet. Blue-and-white police cars appeared every two or three blocks.

The sedan pulled through an iron gate in a tall brick wall, and into a parking lot marked DOCTORS ONLY with a large sign. A hospital administrator in shirt-sleeves was waiting to show them to a space. Dan and Nancy got out and went inside, while the other remained for a moment in the car, talking.

In the shabby lobby she pressed his good hand. "I'll wait down here. They—they'll probably let only one person at a time into the room up there, anyway."

"Listen, Nancy. You do understand why I want to see her. I feel responsible."

"Though you're not. I understand."

"You know I didn't have any real choice about what I was doing."

"I know. I understand."

Whether she did or not, he gave her a kiss, and then he went up on his lonely elevator ride, that delivered him in to a hospital hallway of blue tile and blue paint, a hallway shabby and overused but clean. Above the nurses' outpost was a little sign:

COUNTY HOSPITAL BURNS AND HAND SURGERY UNIT

After they had garbed him in a sterile yellow gown and mask—he needed help to get the garments on, with his slung arm—they pointed out her room, which he would have known anyway from the yellow-gowned guard who stood outside.

When he went in, he saw two beds. No space to spare in here, no private rooms. On one bed, only eyes looked out from a bandaged face, and under a sheet-tent supported on a low frame he caught a glimpse of red-burned flesh unclothed. He had thought no one could live with that much skin destroyed. Maybe no one could. This was a girl, a female anyway, and here she was exposed for casual eyes. It was total exposure but not nakedness. Nakedness was evidently only skin deep, and went when the skin went, sin gone with skin and nothing left to violate.

Wanda was on the other bed, also under a sheet tent. The doctors had said that her burns covered about twenty per cent of her body, but she was out of danger now. Her face was almost unmarked, bearing only two small spots of red destruction. Most of her hair was gone.

"Hello, Wanda."

Her eyes knew him, but his appearance brought no great reaction, of surprise or anything else. Her hands were under the tent, or he would have tried to touch one of them.

"Someone told me you helped to pull me out," she said after a little time.

"You were out of the house. I helped get you away from it before it fell." About all they had told her, he had been warned, was that there had been a fire—as if she didn't already have a firmer grasp than they did of that point. But she knew nothing as yet of the how or why, or that the world had changed with that fire and the events around it, or that her picture with Dan's and others involved was in the newspapers around the world, or that guards from several levels of government were alternately on duty outside her door. It would be another day or two before they started telling her all that.

"Does any of your family come to see you?"

"My mother's been in a couple times. Didn't have much to say."

Neither could Dan find much now. "They tell me this is one of the best places in the world to be if you're burned," he offered at last.

"I don't think there is a best place."

"Listen," he said eventually. "One reason I came

is to tell you I'm very sorry. Another thing is that you shouldn't worry about how any of this is to be paid for, or what you'll do for a job when you get out. I mean it. I've got like this super insurance policy," he suddenly invented. Special Act of Congress, appropriating funds, was the reality. "You won't have to worry a bit about any of that. Really." God, he thought suddenly, I hope she never comes to visit us, never just drops in.

"Your wife come home yet?"

After a while, he had to nod.

When he came out of the hospital with Nancy it was already getting dark. Above the expressway lights, Polaris at the celestial pole was barely visible, but higher in the sky both Mars and giant Antares were fiery bright and red.

FRED SABERHAGEN

THE BEST IN SCIENCE FICTION

THE BEST IN FANTASY

THE BEST IN HORROR